SWEET VIDALIA BRAND

THE OKLAHOMA BRANDS
BOOK SIX

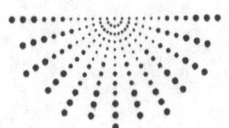

MAGGIE SHAYNE

OLIVERHEBERBOOKS

Copyright © 2014 by Maggie Shayne

Published by Oliver-Heber Books

0 9 8 7 6 5 4 3 2 1

❀ Created with Vellum

THE OKLAHOMA BRANDS

CHAPTER ONE

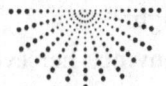

*V*idalia Brand's guilty secret walked in through the batwing doors of the OK Corral and just stood there—tall and lean and more dangerously handsome than he'd been before.

Vidalia was behind the long, gleaming bar, leaning over it to re-tape the draping pine garland that had come loose from the corner, when his dark silhouette appeared. It was almost like she knew it was him just from the way his shadow fell ahead of the street lights behind him. Even before she looked up, a chill ran the length of her spine. Or maybe that was a tingle. And then she straightened up and looked at him. The twinkling holiday lights that decked the saloon fell on his whiskered face, and the end of the pine garland she'd been holding dropped from her hand to hang limply again.

The familiar noise of her beloved saloon—clinking glasses, chinking ice, murmuring conversation—seemed to fall silent as he met her eyes and just stared at her. Vidalia blushed as if she was that young twenty something he'd known a thousand years ago. And she couldn't take her eyes from his, even if she tried.

They were still just as blue—that deep, dark midnight blue that could turn electric with emotion.

If not for Randy Travis's version of *Rockin' Around The Christmas Tree* still coming from the jukebox, you could've heard a pin drop. And she realized every patron she had was looking from her to the stranger and back again. Only he was no stranger. Not to her, he wasn't.

"Miz Brand? You all right?"

She couldn't quite convince her eyes to look at Henry, her come-lately short-order cook, but she did manage to answer him. "Would you stick that garland back up for me, Henry? I can't get it to stay." As she said it, she pulled her apron off, balled it up and shoved it under the bar. Then she walked out from behind it, wondering how she looked, if her hair was wild or her makeup smeared. It didn't matter. She was a working woman, after all. And he was nothing but a brush with disaster from the distant past. He was the man who'd almost ensured her an eternity in Hell. Maybe had.

Before she knew it, she was standing in front of him, having crossed the barroom beneath green and silver garland and strategically placed mistletoe, past dozens of customers who were also friends and neighbors—and busybodies to boot. Maybe some of them spoke to her as she walked by. Maybe she even muttered a response. Damned if she knew.

He was still the same. So tall that she felt diminutive when she stood close to him. He still wore that deliberately rugged, three days growth of whiskers on his face. There was a little gray in it now. Hadn't been before. If anything, it made him seem even sexier.

How could she still feel the same irresistible attraction to him after all these years? Was that even possible? She thought she was long since over this sinfully sexy drifter.

"Hello, Vidalia. It's been a long time." He took off his Stetson, held it by its brim, faked a smile that didn't reach his eyes. His voice was so deep and rich that it felt like he was whispering the words against the skin of her spine, for the shivers that wriggled up and down it.

She decided to test her voice, and tried to make it come out firm and casual, not whispery soft with longing and remembered bliss. "Hello Bobby. What the hell are you doing here?"

His eyes widened a little, then he smiled and this time it seemed a little more genuine. "You still cut straight through the bull, don't you Vidalia? You haven't changed a bit, except to get prettier."

"And you still cut straight *to* the bull. You haven't changed either."

He held up both hands as if in surrender. "I'm in Big Falls on business. I had to stop by and say hello."

"Well, now you have." A thousand questions sprang to mind, questions she fought hard not to ask. Like, what sort of business could he possibly have here in the small town of Big Falls, Oklahoma? He'd gone from being a handy man back when she'd known him to a billionaire businessman. He'd made a fortune buying up failing saloons, turning them into successful tourist traps and then selling them at a profit. But there were no failing saloons in Big Falls. There were a couple of dive bars, and there was the OK Corral. "So hello, Bobby Joe. And Goodbye."

His face fell, those heavy dark brows bending a little in the center. God, he was even handsome when he frowned. "Why so hostile, Vidalia? It's been—"

"I know *exactly* how long it's been." She bit her lip and sent a quick glance around her to see a lot of interested eyes still turned in their direction. Lowering her voice, she brushed past him, through the batwing doors and outside. He came too, and she saw him push the outer door closed behind him. Good. They should be closed.

It was a cool night in Big Falls. Late December. Almost Christmas. They might even get a snowflake or two this year.

Nothing like the year of the blizzard, but maybe.... Snow at Christmas was something she prayed for every year, but those prayers were rarely answered. Well, they were, but the answer was usually no.

She hugged her arms and watched her breath emerge in puffs of steam as she walked along the front of the building, away from the welcoming holiday lights, past the wreath-decked windows to a shadowy corner. The stars were twinkling from a wide, clear sky. He came up behind her, and she made herself face him. "I don't mean to be hostile. You were...you and me, we were a mistake Bobby. A mistake that could've cost me dearly."

"I think the only mistake we made back then was denying what we both wanted."

She shot him her patented glare. "I was a married woman."

"You only thought you were married. You didn't know he was a bigamist who'd married another woman before you. You were all alone, trying to start up a business and raise four girls by yourself. Working yourself into the ground while he was out spending time with his other family. If I'd known that then, I'd have never left."

She let him rant. John deserved it, and worse. But when Bobby finished cursing her late husband, she looked at him very calmly and said, "It wouldn't have made a difference if you'd known. Or even if I'd known. I said vows in front of God in a church full of witnesses. Just because he didn't keep his, that didn't free me from mine. When I make a promise, I keep it."

He lowered his head. "I know. I know that about you."

She sighed, unsure what the point was of dragging all this up now. "What are you doing back here, Bobby?"

He heaved a heavy sigh. "Like I said, business. I couldn't be here and not come by. Just to see you. Just to say...I never forgot."

He was looking into her eyes. His were just as deep and

expressive as she remembered. They'd stared into hers on the dance floor of this very saloon. Only it had been empty, the chairs all tipped up on top of the tables, the lights down low. They'd kept on dancing long after the last song on the jukebox had stopped playing. And then he'd kissed her, and then....

She looked at his lips, just as thick and soft as before, and had to close her eyes to block the memory out.

His voice was hoarse when he spoke again. Almost as if he, too, had been remembering that night so long ago. "Have dinner with me, Vidalia? Just to catch up. I promise I won't bring up the past if you don't want me to."

"I don't think that's a good idea, Bobby."

His disappointment showed in his eyes, just like every emotion always did, and it made her feel mean. "Why not? You're not a married woman anymore. You've got no vows to keep."

She lowered her head so he wouldn't see how tempted she was to say yes. Tempted. That was the word, wasn't it? He had been her biggest temptation. Her test, maybe. A test she'd failed miserably. She wasn't so sure she'd be any more successful this time, no matter how much older and wiser and stronger she was.

"I really can't, Bobby," she said. "But it was nice to see you. Good luck with your business, whatever it is."

She walked past him, back to the saloon's big door, hoping he wouldn't follow and make a scene. Or more of a scene than he'd already caused, because she had no doubt the tongues were wagging. By tomorrow morning, the Big Falls grapevine would resemble a burning bush. And there wasn't a thing she could do about it.

She went through the door, and for some perverse reason, left it open behind her as she pushed on through the batwings. Then she paused just inside the saloon. The Christmas music was still going, glasses were still clinking, and people had resumed their conversations. She wanted to turn around, to see if he'd followed, or if he was leaving, but she stiffened her spine and walked right back to the bar, smiling and chatting with customers on the way. She felt his eyes on her from behind, but only briefly. And then she heard the sound of a large motor, probably a pickup truck. Probably his.

Closing her eyes, stiffening her spine, she told herself she'd done the right thing. The hard thing, yes, but the right thing. This time.

～

Bobby Joe McIntyre drove his pickup truck as far as the giant Christmas tree in the center of town. The forty-foot blue spruce was all decked out in twinkling lights against one of the darkest nights he could recall. There had been stars before, when he'd been standing outside the OK Corral with Vidalia, but clouds had blown in and not a single star looked down at him now. It was like they'd all gone out three months ago when his charmed life had come crashing down around him. He'd thought maybe seeing Vidalia again might reignite at least a couple of the luminaries that used to favor him. And it had, for a few precious seconds. But she'd shot him down, added a bucket of ice water to the star-dousing party.

It had been years ago, but he remembered it like it was yesterday.

He'd been a single, hardworking handyman. She'd been a married mother of four girls with a husband who was perpetually absent. She'd bought an abandoned motel for back taxes and hired him to help her turn it into a saloon. The OK corral.

She'd been something else back then. Hell, she still was. All of five foot two, with curves that probably still drew appreciative looks from every red-blooded male in town. He was no exception. Rich, lustrous curls as black as ebony wood, and the

6

most fiery brown eyes ever to flash his way. Lashes like velvet fringe. Skin like caramel satin.

He'd admired her. Her work ethic. Her no-nonsense attitude. Her temper. Her steadfast morality. And the passion he sensed bubbling like a cauldron over a low flame—passion neglected by the man whose job it was to tend it. She kept that cauldron covered up tight.

They'd worked late the night before the OK Corral's grand opening, unpacking glasses and bottles of liquor, stocking the kitchen and the shelves. By then he knew two things for sure: She had no intention of breaking her marriage vows, and she wanted him just as bad as he wanted her.

"How about a toast?" he'd asked. "To celebrate your dream coming true?"

She'd smiled—that killer smile he had never managed to get out of his head in all these years. Then she went behind the bar to pour them each a shot of top-shelf whiskey.

He'd walked over to the brand new jukebox–the same one that had been playing country Christmas songs tonight–dropped a nickel into the slot, and chose *Lead Me On*, by Conway and Loretta. He'd never forgotten the way she'd looked as she'd come around the bar with a drink in each hand, pretending not to notice the lyrics. Beautiful. Tempted. And scared.

She handed him a glass. "To the best little saloon in Oklahoma," she said, lifting her own.

He lifted his too. "And to the prettiest saloon owner in the entire U S of A." He tapped the rim of his glass to the rim of hers and downed the whiskey in a single gulp. She only sipped from hers. And then he said, "Break in the dance floor with me, Vidalia?"

She lowered her eyes a little. "I should get on home. The girls–"

"Are sound asleep by now. So's the sitter, I'll bet. They won't

7

notice if you're five minutes later." He took her glass from her, set it on the bar beside his. "C'mon, Vi. You've worked hard. *We've* worked hard. We deserve to celebrate, even if it's just with one dance." He held out his arms.

Sighing, she went into them. "Just one dance," she said. "And that's all."

"That's all."

But when she moved up close to him, and he lowered his arms around her waist, he couldn't help the sheer male pleasure that filled him. The scent of her perfume reached him. Vanilla and something else. Something just slightly spicy and exotic. Her body was just barely touching his, and he wanted to press her closer, but knew she'd probably slap the lust right off his face if he did. So he settled for the soft, accidental brushing of breasts to chest, and thigh to thigh every now and then.

She rested her hands on his shoulders, didn't close them around his neck the way he wanted her to. But he didn't push. He settled for that. They'd spent hours together, for months on end while she'd worked her perfect backside off and put every spare penny into the saloon. She'd insisted on paying him for the work he did, even though he'd offered more than once to do it for nothing. Just being around her was payment enough.

And finally the work was done, and he would have no more excuses to be with her all the time, alone, late at night. No more reason. And he knew her too well to think she might give him one.

This was a goodbye dance. And he was pretty sure she knew that as well as he did.

And then the song ended, and a miracle happened. She tipped her head up, looked right into his eyes and let him see, just for a second, the feelings she kept so closely guarded.

He couldn't help himself. He lowered his head, and he caught her mouth with his, and she didn't pull away. No, she kissed him back, her arms twisting tight around his neck to pull herself up higher. His heart took off like a racehorse at the sound of the starter's pistol, and he bent over her, holding her body tight to his just like he'd been wanting to. He kissed her deeply, leaving no doubt in her mind that he'd like to do a lot more.

She kissed him right back, just as full of enthusiasm as he was. And when he finally lifted his head, wondering where they would go to do what seemed inevitable, she looked deeply into his eyes, and hers were wet.

"Are you...crying?"

"Not yet." She put her hands on his shoulders, and firmly held them there while she took a step back. "I'm a married woman, Bobby."

"Don't I know it."

She nodded. "Then you know this has to stop right here. I shouldn't have even...." Closing her eyes, lowering her head, she said no more. Just walked over to the juke box and pulled the plug. Then she picked up her shot glass, downed its contents in a gulp. "I'm not the cheatin' kind, Bobby. I'd hate myself if I did something like that."

And right then, he felt the truth of those words. "I guess I know that, too."

"You ought to. You oughtta know it better than most anyone in this town."

He nodded, wanted to argue, to reason, to rationalize, but he did know her better than anyone, and he knew that if he made love to Vidalia Brand, he would be destroying her at the very same time. He couldn't do that to her.

"I'm leaving town tomorrow, Vidalia," he said. And he hadn't known he was going to say it until he did.

"Don't feel like you have to—"

"I have to." He sighed. "I've got some money saved up. There's a falling down Cantina just this side of the Tex-Mex border going up for auction."

9

Her head came up, eyes lighting, her smile genuine. "You're goin' into the saloon business?"

"Not like you, but yeah, that's the plan."

"You're gonna do well, Bobby," she told him. "And I'm not ashamed to say, I'm gonna miss you."

"I'm gonna miss you too," he told her. And he thought he meant it a whole lot more than she did.

She held his eyes for a long time, and then she went behind the bar and refilled both their glasses.

That had been twenty-some-odd years ago. And that whole time, he'd never been able to get past the notion that Vidalia Brand was The One. The only woman for him. And for some reason, he just wasn't meant to have her. Not in this lifetime, anyway.

Maybe next time around, he thought as he stood there looking up at the red and green and blue and white lights of the giant Christmas tree. If there was a next time. He wasn't the sort of man who had any real convictions about what happened after you died. But he supposed he'd be finding out firsthand in short order. Any time now, according to his doctors.

He sighed heavily, and his breath made a steam puff in the darkness. Then he got back into his pickup and turned it around, driving back toward the former feed store he'd bought at the far end of town. He had the entire thing draped in an exterminator's tent, so the work going on inside would go unseen until he was ready to make it public day after tomorrow.

He'd made a fortune taking over failing bars, saloons and nightclubs, recreating them into successful hot spots, and then selling them for massive profits. He'd become one of the richest men in Texas. He'd married, had three sons, and neglected them almost as much as John Brand had neglected his daughters. He'd divorced after fifteen years with a woman he had liked at first, disliked later on, but never loved. There was only one woman he'd ever really loved.

It was only a month ago that he'd realized he wanted to leave something more behind than a portfolio stuffed with paper wealth. He wanted to leave his sons something real. Something of him. Something they could be proud of. And he wanted it to be in Big Falls Oklahoma, where he'd been a young man with his entire future ahead of him, who didn't yet know that he'd never be happier than he was right then. Richer. More successful. Busier. But never happier.

Seeing Vidalia again had been a bonus to coming back here. But it hadn't been his only reason. He intended to breathe his last in Big Falls, the closest thing to a hometown he'd ever had.

But his main reason for coming back here now was because he wanted to spend one more Christmas in Big Falls. Christmases had been magical here. Vidalia and her little girls always made them so special, even when he'd just been a lonely drifter handyman with no family to call his own. Three Christmases, he'd been invited to share in the holiday meal with the Brands. Three Christmases when John Brand had seen fit to be elsewhere. Even poor, Vidalia had given her girls holidays to remember. Meaningful, sparkling, magical holidays full of love and laughter.

He wanted his boys to experience a holiday like those ones he remembered, just once. He'd been too busy getting rich to give them any of those. And according to his doctors, he should just about have enough time left to make that happen.

CHAPTER TWO

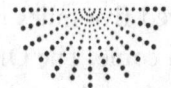

*a*n hour later, after closing time, Vidalia stood in the cold rain, looking across Main Street at what used to be Milner Feed & Grain. The big building was wearing an "I'm being exterminated" sort of disguise. Maybe it really was an exterminator's tent covering the entire place. Vidalia wouldn't know, having never seen one. Bugs only tended to be a problem in big cities, where there wasn't room for them to live outdoors where they belonged. She'd seen big city life. Never lived it. If she had, she figured she'd have most likely run screaming for this particular corner of Oklahoma. The northwestern part, where there were mountains, and where there was weather. They got a little snow once or twice over the course of an average winter. She wondered again if they would this year. Snow for Christmas...that would be something, wouldn't it?

She almost asked God to send her some, but then she couldn't quite do it. She'd sinned. She'd sinned in a big way, and she had never made that sin right. And while she'd managed to push it to the back of her mind for a good many years, it was front and center, now. She didn't feel she had any business asking God for anything.

13

Sighing, she pushed the dark thoughts aside and got back to the moment at hand. There wasn't a lick of traffic on the slick, shiny ribbon of road that unfurled in either direction. The sheen of rain on the blacktop was the only way to tell the difference between the road and the night itself. There wasn't another car around, either. And she'd left her own a football field away, before she'd got here. The former feed store was right on the edge of town. Vidalia lived five miles beyond the other end of town, back the way she'd come. The OK Corral, her best friend for the past more-years-than-she-cared-to-count, was on the opposite end of Main.

Her hair was getting wet. She should've brought a hat. But she hadn't had one with her at the Corral, and she'd come directly here from there. Probably because she was afraid she'd lose her nerve if she went home first. It would be too easy to just go to bed and try to forget about....

About Bobby.

Not that she would've been able to.

Nope, Bobby Joe McIntyre was on her mind. And in her town. And it hadn't taken too much algebra to figure out why. He'd made his millions buying out saloons, rebuilding them into something huge and gaudy and soulless, and then selling them again. There were no out of business saloons in Big Falls. Not right now, anyway. But there was one former feed store, auctioned off for taxes months ago, that had suddenly come to life underneath an oversized tent. And there were strangers in town. Oh, they were careful, showing up only a few at a time to shop or use the Post Office. But there were a lot of them. She'd been keeping track. No less than twenty new faces had appeared on the other side of her mahogany bar in the past few weeks. Working men, hardly a female among 'em.

Until she'd seen Bobby, she'd assumed it was some PR stunt by whatever corporate giant was going to try to put up a chain

14

store where the feed and grain used to be. There'd been good-natured debate among the locals about what it would be.

But the minute she'd seen Bobby's still sinfully sexy backside walking away, it had hit her. It was a saloon. That was his business. Big, flashy, city-slickin', modern mockeries of old west clichés. He was in this town to put her out of business.

And playing on that one night, and what had happened between them—almost happened, as far as he would ever know—to keep her too flustered to notice what was happening right under her nose.

She would be damned if she was going to take this sitting down.

But of course, she had to make sure.

Drawing a deep breath, she hunched her shoulders, stepped out from under the leafless tree that she'd been trying to use as an umbrella, and jogged across Main Street and around to one side of the building. Then she stood there with her back against the canvas tent, looking at the night and the parking lot and the road.

It was quiet as a churchyard and cold enough to raise goose bumps on the Devil's backside.

Okay, it's now or never.

The main entrance to the feed and grain used to be right about where she was standing. So she crouched low, lifted the tent, and ducked underneath. And then she stood there between the brown slab wood siding and the canvas, fumbling in her jacket pocket for the flashlight she'd brought from the saloon.

The main entrance was no longer where it had been or it would've been in front her nose. She shone the light up and down the siding, and realized by its gleam that it wasn't wood at all. It was some kind of plastic made to look like slab wood. Didn't that just figure? Make believe wood for a make believe saloon, if her theory panned out.

She moved the flashlight further until it gleamed on a great big window a few feet away. So she edged that way, thinking that from the outside she must look like a giant tick on a barn-sized hound dog.

There, now she was in front of the big window. She cupped her hands around either side of her face and tried to see inside, then had to cup the flashlight in one fist and press it flush against the glass to light the inside a little bit. But its beam didn't go far enough.

She was frowning, squinting, and frustrated, when she heard the distinct sound of a shotgun working a shell into the chamber. Pump-action, if she wasn't mistaken. And she wasn't.

"All right, Mister, I've got you in my sights," Bobby said. "You come on out from behind that canvas nice and slow. And put your hands up just as quick as you can manage. Understood?"

"Yeah," she said. And she didn't waste a lot of time obeying.

She lifted the tarp and poked her head out from underneath it, and before she even got upright, was blinded by a flashlight beam.

"Vidalia? Is that you?"

She pressed her lips. "Yeah, Bobby, it's me. Put the light down, will you? Shotgun too, if the barrel's still pointed my way."

"Son of a—"

"Watch the language, Bobby."

The flashlight moved away, but the damage was done. She was blinking like a mole as his long, tall silhouette strode across the street toward her. Bastard was wearing a duster, of all things. A duster and that Stetson from earlier. He couldn't have a little mercy? She was ashamed but wasn't about to hang her head because of it. God knew she'd done worse things. That was the problem.

She kept her chin high, looked him right in the eyes when she could finally see them.

"You care to tell me what you're doin', sneakin' around my place in the middle of the night, Vidalia?"

He'd never called her Vi. Always Vidalia. She'd loved that about him. "You just answered your own question."

"Huh?" The light came up again. She blocked her eyes with a hand and he lowered it.

"What am I doin'? I'm sneaking around your place in the middle of the night."

"Don't be a smartass."

She shrugged. "I figured out what you were up to as soon as you left the Corral and my head stopped spinning."

His even, white smile appeared so suddenly she thought he'd turned the flashlight back on. "I made your head spin?"

"Don't change the subject. I know what you're up to, Bobby. I just came out here to make sure. Figured I should give you the benefit of the doubt till I'd seen proof."

"So this is you giving me the benefit of the doubt."

She nodded, standing her ground. Her ridiculous-sounding, but utterly true ground.

"You could've just asked me what I was doing in town, you know."

"I asked you. Twice. You gave me a non-answer both times." She shrugged and reached the spot where he stood, looking up into the rain and into his eyes.

He took off his Stetson and put it on her head. "Ask me again."

"What are you doing in town?"

He took his time about looking at her face before he finally nodded, twice, slow. "Didn't you see?"

"Nope. You started bellering at me just as I got a good look through that window. Scared me so bad I almost dropped my flashlight." She looked at him, looked close, just as he'd done to her. Her eyes had finally adjusted, so she could see the cut of his jaw. It was a really nice jaw, wide and square, although at the moment it was set a little tightly for her taste.

"Can I buy you a drink, Vidalia Brand?"

"Corral's closed."

"I know." He took her by the elbow and led her toward the front of the place. Then he unzipped a doorway in the canvas and led her through, and then through a great big set of double arching doors behind it.

The entryway was huge, with coatracks and benches, and dead center, a set of batwing doors that put her own to shame, their wood all tooled and then the cuts painted gold. Some would call it elaborate. She would call it gaudy.

That was when she knew she'd been right. And he left her for a moment, and went through them. Flipping a switch, he flooded the place with light.

Vidalia pushed through the swinging doors and took a long, slow look around. There were round tables, antiqued to look old. There were chandeliers made out of elk racks. There was a three sided hardwood bar three times as long as the one in the OK Corral, with high standing saddle shaped seats all the way around. It was backed by a mirror the entire length of it, behind racks and shelves for bottles and glasses and pitchers. There was a pizza slice shaped stage at the front right corner of the place, a dance floor the size of a basketball court. Half of one anyway. And the coolest mechanical bull over in the corner.

And beside the stage, a player piano. It looked like an antique, not a replica. Wow.

She didn't know whether to tell him how amazing the place was or kick the man where he would know he'd been kicked.

Instead, she turned and looked up and right into his eyes, put her hands on her hips and tapped one foot, awaiting his explanation.

~

Bobby couldn't think straight with Vidalia's big brown eyes looking up into his. Her expression was probably supposed to be fierce, but all he wanted to do was kiss it right off her pretty face. God, he'd missed her, ached for her, though he'd buried it so deep it had just become a vague sense of dissatisfaction with everything in his life. His marriage, his sons, his wealth. No matter how much he did, it was never enough to fill the hole she'd left in his heart.

"It's...a saloon," he said.

"I can *see* it's a saloon," she replied. "Of sorts."

"I'm calling it The Long Branch."

"No one under fifty even remembers *Gunsmoke* anymore, Bobby."

"That makes it even better. A little obscure. The kind of thing the kids will Google."

"It's a second saloon in a one-saloon town. You came here to put me out of business."

"Don't be ridiculous. Hell, come 'ere." He walked her across the big dance floor toward the stage. There were red velvet curtains on either side of it, held back by golden cords. "The OK Corral is a place for the locals, where they can relax and drink and get some bar food at great prices. You agree with that description?"

She pursed her lips, lowered her head, saying nothing, not giving him an inch.

"The Long Branch is more of a tourist attraction."

"We don't have tourism in Big Falls. Has it really been so long you don't know that?"

"They have tourism in Tucker Lake, and that's only a few miles east. And there are a half dozen Ghost Towns within a seventy-mile radius, all of them doing steady business. This is gonna become a regular stop for those same tourists. It'll bring business to everyone in Big Falls, you included. We're gonna have floor shows, waitresses dressed as saloon girls. Every now and then we'll have some actors come in and shoot the place up, then be rounded up and arrested by a Marshall Dillon type. Lots of special effects to make it seem real. You know how some places do mystery dinners? We'll be doing Dime Novel dinners. And I mean full dinners, with a well-staffed kitchen and one of the best chefs in the state. Here, take a look at the menu." He took hold of her arm, but she tugged it away as he led her back to the bar. He walked around behind it, plucked a menu from a stack, and set it, open, in front of her.

She sighed, but slid up onto a saddle shaped barstool and looked down at the menu. Then she blinked slow and looked up at him again. "I can't really–"

"Here. Use mine." He'd already had his bifocals in hand, and he set them on top of the menu.

She picked them up, red in the cheeks—which was a good look on her, he thought. Then she put them on and looked at the menu. He did too. And he didn't need his glasses, because he knew it by heart. Cowboy burgers. Six-gun steaks. Great big racks of ribs with the sweetest, tangiest barbeque sauce he'd ever tasted. Fried chicken. Mashed potatoes and gravy. It was old fashioned food, stick to the ribs food. Cowboy food. Food they didn't serve far and wide anymore. But prepared by a gourmet chef with prices befitting his skill.

She shifted her eyes a little, then they widened. "Your prices are on the uppity side, don't you think?"

"Like I said, I'm not trying to compete with you. The floor show's free. But we gotta cover expenses."

She closed the menu, slid it back across the bar to him. "Still and all, it doesn't change what you did. You flattered me. Turned my head, to be honest. I'm ashamed to admit it, but I'm not in the habit of ducking the truth. I was feeling giddy as a school girl when you gave me those cow eyes and pretended you'd been missing me all these years. But it was just some two bit, side-winding dirty trick." She slid off the stool. It was a little drop to the floor, but she managed to make it with dignity.

"Um, you shot me down, Vidalia."

"Well what earthly difference does *that* make?"

She started walking toward the front door.

Thinking fast, Bobby grabbed the remote from its holster on the inside edge of the bar, aimed and fired. The lights dropped down low, the bulbs taking on a flickering quality, like gas lamps. She stopped walking, looking around in surprise. He hit another button and music came up—Conway and Loretta singing *Lead Me On*. And Vidalia turned toward him with a "You don't think that's gonna work, do you?" expression on her pretty face.

He jumped up onto the bar, sliding on his denim clad back-side right across it, and jumping clean off the other side. Then he strode right up to her, slid one arm around her waist, and clasped her hand in the other one.

"What do you think you're doing?" She didn't pull away.

"Aside from pulling a hamstring with that bar-jumping thing I just did to impress you, you mean?"

She tried not to smile. She was fighting it with everything in her. "Yeah, aside from that."

"I'm testing out my new dance floor." He nudged her into motion, and she fell right into step with him, following his steps without a single falter. So he got a little fancy, giving her a spin, followed by a dip, then pulling her back up again and holding her a little closer than before.

She laughed when he did that. Tipped her head back and laughed, and when she brought her eyes to his again, he got stuck there. This was magical, what was sparkling between the two of them, he thought. It was just like that night so long ago.

And then he remembered his situation. This wasn't fair to her.

The song ended, and he let her go. "I'm real sorry I offended you, Vidalia. And I admit, I did walk into the Corral with the intention of asking for your advice and assistance with this new venture of mine. But the minute I saw you again, it wasn't business at all anymore."

She lowered her head, and he couldn't tell in the dim light, but he thought she was thinking.

"Your dance floor works just fine," she said at length. "I can't remember the last time I waltzed around a barroom."

"I remember the last time I did," he said. "With you, in the Corral. To that same song."

She shot him a look and he knew she remembered as well as he did. Maybe she was surprised that he did, though.

His conscience pricked him, reminding him to be careful. It wouldn't be fair to lead her on. To let her see how much he wanted to pull her close and dance another round. Or two. Or all night long.

"I wish you good luck with the, uh, The Long Branch." She looked at his face for a long time. "You're a charmer, Bobby Joe McIntyre. But it didn't work."

"It didn't?"

"No. I'm gonna do everything I can do to put you out of business. Because the OK Corral is my baby. The only one that didn't grow up and leave the nest. She's all I've got in the world right now, and I'm not about to let you come waltzing into town and ruin her."

"I don't want to ruin the Corral, Vidalia."

"This is a one-saloon town. I'm gonna make sure that one saloon is always the OK Corral."

He lowered his head. "All right then. If that's how it has to be."

"That's how it is." She nodded once and started for the door.

"Thanks for the dance," he called after her.

"You're welcome." She reached the batwing doors, pushed

through them, stopped on the other side, and looked back at him. "So, um...you want to get together for lunch tomorrow?"

He smiled real slow. "You're damn straight I do."

She smiled back at him. Damn, she was one Class-A beauty when she smiled. Then she turned and walked out the door, leaving him to wonder just what the hell he thought he was doing.

CHAPTER THREE

"*I*'ve been so busy with life lately, Mom. The twins and Caleb and all. I feel like I've been neglecting you."

Vidalia raised her eyebrows at her eldest daughter and continued sipping coffee from her favorite mug. It had a sexy cowboy on it, whose shirt vanished as the coffee level went down. Melusine had bought it for her last Christmas as part of the girls' ongoing, good natured battle over who could get their mother the best present. Of course, Maya had won by delivering the twins on Christmas four years ago, and then Kara had tied her by bringing little Tyler into the family two Christmasses later. But Vidalia didn't mind that they all kept trying. Mel's mug certainly made the morning cuppa more interesting, and as a bonus, it discouraged that second cup Vidalia probably shouldn't have. After all, you didn't want to put the cowboy's shirt back *on*.

Carefully, she set the mug on the kitchen table. "You haven't been neglecting me at all, hon. We see each other every day."

"I know, but we haven't really talked, except about the kids."

She sipped her own coffee from a far less interesting mug, and said, "How are things with you, Mom? Anything...new?"

Subtle, she wasn't. "Don't beat around the bush, Maya. You're too old for that. Just tell me what's on your mind."

Maya didn't return her steady gaze. She looked past her instead, into the living room where the twins were playing with the plethora of toys Vidalia kept on hand, but eyeing the ornaments on the giant balsam fir tree as if they would far prefer to play with those.

"I heard a stranger came into the Corral last night."

"Strangers come into the Corral every night." She wasn't going to make this easy on her firstborn. Vidalia was an adult woman and she didn't need supervision from her offspring. And yes, she was feeling very defensive about this. About Bobby Joe. And for good reasons that were her own fault and not Maya's. Still, she couldn't help bristling a little.

"I heard you went outside to talk to him. And that you seemed...flustered."

Vidalia shrugged. "I wouldn't say flustered is the right word. And he's not a stranger. He's Bobby Joe McIntyre."

"So who is he? What's going on?"

"You mean you don't remember him?" Vidalia asked.

"No." Maya tilted her head and frowned. "Should I?"

Shrugging, Vidalia examined the now half-naked cowboy on her mug and thought Bobby looked better. He'd looked better then, and he still looked better to her. She'd always had a weakness for that man.

"He used to be a local." Vidalia shrugged as if it didn't much matter. "He bought the old feed & grain place, and he's turning it into a big glitzy tourist trap he calls a saloon."

Maya blinked, maybe not expecting the answer she got. "So...you don't *know* him."

"Oh, I *know* him." Vidalia got up from the table and went to the coffee pot on the counter for a refill. Never mind that it put the cowboy's shirt back on. She'd take it off again in short order. "He was my handyman, back when you and your sisters were still young enough to respect your mama's privacy. You must've been about six. He and I turned a run-down motel into the OK Corral on a shoestring budget with nothing much more than elbow grease and determination."

Maya frowned as if trying to remember. Vidalia thought she might if she gave her a few more clues, but she wasn't sure she wanted to. "What's this guy's name again?" she asked.

"Bobby Joe...that is Jason Robert Joseph McIntyre."

"Jason Robert Jos....JRJ McIntyre? The Texas Billionaire?" Her eyes were bigger than an Oklahoma harvest moon just then.

Vidalia just shrugged. "He was no billionaire back in the day," she said, thinking back. "Poor as a church mouse, and pretty much alone in the world. We had him over for Christmas dinner two years in a row. Maybe three. And he brought you gifts every time. Remember those little rag dolls with the black button eyes you all got one year? And there were four pairs of shiny black patent leather shoes another. He even got the sizes right."

Maya was frowning. "Four...then it was before Selene came along?"

Vidalia got up from the table and wandered to the sink to dump out that second cup she shouldn't have poured. "Must've been. Who can remember?"

"Sounds like you remember it pretty well."

She didn't look back around at her daughter, probably because she was afraid Maya might see her guilty secret in her eyes.

"So you and he were...close."

Vidalia turned then, and speared Maya with her eyes. "Just what are you asking me, daughter?"

"I just...I thought you and Caleb's dad–"

"Caleb's father is a city slicker, born and bred. You can't possibly think that was ever going to go where he wanted it to."

"So you're saying it's not?"

"Of course not. And since when do you get to ask me questions about my love life, Maya?"

"Love life? Jeeze, Mom, up until now I didn't even know you *had* a love life."

Vidalia bit back the urge to tell her daughter that whether she did or not, it was none of her business. They were a close family. And if she were honest, she would admit she'd dished out the same kind of third degree she was now being served with each of the girls. But she did not need and would not seek her offsprings' approval when it came to...feelings like the ones Bobby stirred up in her. Feelings she was too ashamed of to even talk about with her minister, much less her kids.

"Mom, did this guy mean something to you?"

Vidalia lowered her head. "I was a married woman."

"Not legally, you weren't."

She shook her head. "It's been more than twenty years. It's ancient history that doesn't matter in the least anymore." She looked in at the twins. "They're trying to peel the plastic off the candy candes with their teeth, Maya. Best take them home and feed them."

The five concerned daughters of Vidalia Brand met at Edie and Wade's gorgeous place overlooking the falls, because it was the farthest from home. Vidalia's big farmhouse would always be "home" to them. Maya had called the meeting, but Edie had been about to, and she wasted no time getting to the point once they were all gathered around the giant Christmas tree in her living room. It went clear up to the cathedral ceiling and filled the front window. Breathtaking, Edie thought. She loved her home. Sally, the Great Dane, lay on the floor in front of the tree, her favorite spot, and sighed repeatedly to convey how much she hated being mauled by children. Yet she didn't get up and leave, and she didn't growl, and every once in a while her tail thumped the floor. The fraud.

"So," Edie began, "Mom's pickup truck was parked alongside Main Street last night, way out at the edge of town in the middle of nowhere. It was after closing time, so you know it was the wee hours. I heard it was there for a while, too. Who knows what's going on?"

The others frowned and lowered their heads, but, Edie noticed, Maya looked alarmed. "Heck," she said with a look at her twins, who were playing with Sally's dog toys, while Tyler, older and wiser and no longer wearing braces on his legs, stroked the dog's head slow and lovingly. "Was it anywhere near the old Feed & Grain?"

"Yeah. In fact, that was the only thing nearby, according to Sunny from the bakery," Edie said. "Why?"

Maya sighed. "Something's up with Mom. Some handsome stranger came into the Corral last night, and she got all worked up, ended up going outside with him for a while."

"Mom did that?" Selene asked, her eyes wide and searching each of her older siblings' faces.

"Go, Mom," Mel muttered. Kara just smiled to herself.

Maya said, "I asked her about it this morning, and she got all defensive and tight lipped. But she did tell me who he was. JRJ McIntyre. Though she calls him Bobby Joe. He was her handyman back when we were little. Helped her change the Corral from an old motel into a saloon."

"Maya, that had to have been more than twenty years ago," Kara said.

Melusine pulled out her phone and started tapping keys. "Funny. Google says RJR McIntyre is a billionaire tycoon from Dallas. Must be a different one. How does he spell–"

"That's the one," Maya said. "She said he was poor back then. And that he came to Christmas at our house a few times."

"The Raggedy Anne Dolls!" Kara all but shouted. "I *do* remember him." She tipped her head sideways. "He always seemed kind of sad to me. Cool that he went out and got all rich and famous."

"He's famous," Edie agreed, "but not for much more than being rich."

"I don't remember him," Selene said, frowning.

"It was before you were born, Selene," Maya went on. "But that's beside the point. I don't care who he is or who he was or how many dolls he bought us when we were kids. He's back in town, and there's something going on between him and Mom. I think we need to find out just what the son of a gun is up to. What his intentions are." Maya got up and paced to the tree, taking an ornament out of CC's hand and putting it back on its branch. "Look, but don't touch, okay kids?"

"They're not gonna break anything, sis," Edie said. "And if they did, I wouldn't care."

"Your home belongs in a magazine, Edie. I'm not gonna risk it."

Mel sighed. "I'll talk to Alex. We're the P.I.s in the family. So it stands to reason we're the ones who should dig into this guy a little bit."

"I don't think that's a good idea at all," Kara said.

"Be discreet," Maya said, almost as if Kara hadn't said a word. Edie saw Kara notice and frown. "Mom's super sensitive about this for some reason," she went on. "She finds out we were snooping, there's gonna be hell to pay."

"We're professionals, Maya. We do this for a living. We know how to be discreet."

"I'll consult the Tarot," Selene said.

"Um, why don't we just talk to Mom," Kara asked.

"I tried that, Kara. She's not talking."

"Well, maybe that's because it's not our business."

They all went silent, staring at Kara with their mouths open. Then they almost jointly shook their heads and resumed the discussion. All except for Selene, who met Kara's eyes and gave a subtle nod to let her know she agreed with her.

∼

"Damn, woman. You look like you just stepped off a cloud, hung up your halo, and came down to visit with an undeserving sinner."

Bobby Joe had always been a charmer. Vidalia met him at Haggerty House, the best restaurant in Tucker Lake, a short drive from Big Falls. As an added benefit, it wasn't very busy at lunch hour. But it was nice. A giant old Victorian house that had been converted to a lush restaurant that served the best meals in a thirty-mile radius. There was a bar off one side, but not like the Corral. It was more a place for folks to get drinks while waiting for a table, than a place to hang out after a hard day's work.

Vidalia liked it here because she identified with its owners. Betty Jean Haggerty had been running the place for as long as anyone could remember, and she had five beautiful grand-daughters who helped her. The girls were near the ages of Vidalia's own brood. No wonder she loved it here.

Besides, family business was family business. They had to support each other. The restaurant's tall, ornate windows looked out over manicured lawns that were not at their prettiest just now, all brown and barren. Vidalia thought again of snow. Second time in as many days.

There were only a few other people in the place, and she didn't know any of them—thank you, Lord. Bobby had been standing near the hostess booth when she'd walked in. And he looked good enough to make her knees buckle with his faded jeans and shiny boots. His shirt was black with pearl snaps, just like the one on her favorite coffee mug, which filled her head with the kinds of thoughts she hadn't had about a man in quite a long time.

Dang.

"I just paid you a compliment, lady. Aren't you even going to thank me?"

"I was gonna, but you distracted me. You look pretty good yourself, cowboy. So where are we sitting?"

"I thought I'd let you pick."

She shrugged, finally noticing the hostess who stood nearby with menus in one hand. She was young, pretty, and familiar. Frowning, Vidalia said, "Wait, wait, I've got this. You're Bridget!"

The girl flashed a bright smile. "Hello again, Ms. Brand. It's been too long." Then she looked at Bobby and there was an expectant pause.

"Oh. Um, this is Bobby Joe. He's an old friend, back in town on business."

"Nice to meet you Bobby Joe," Bridget said. "Any friend of the Brands is a friend of ours. Where would you two like to sit? Pretty much all the tables are up for grabs this early in the day."

"Near the fireplace," Vidalia returned. "This time of year, that's the best view anyway."

"Right this way." And then she turned, taking Vidalia by the arm and leaving Bobby Joe to follow behind them. Leaning in close, she whispered, "Don't take it wrong, but you two look like the perfect couple."

"You inherited your grandma's matchmaking genes, I see," Vidalia said. "How is Betty Jean anyway?"

"Fine, fit, and cooking up a storm. She's gonna be so tickled when I tell her you're here." Bridget put the menus down on the table as Bobby Joe hurried around her to pull out Vidalia's chair. She sat down, and then he sat across from her.

"I'll bring you back some drinks. What would you like?" Bridget asked.

"Beer. Whatever you have on tap."

"Just got a new keg from a local microbrewery that's been getting rave reviews from the customers," Bridget said.

"Okie-Gold?" Vidalia asked.

Bridget winked at her. "That's the one. Should I make it two?"

Not after what happened the last time she and Bobby Joe drank together, she thought. "Uh, no. Tea. A nice cup of hot tea will do me just fine."

"All right. I'll be back." Bridget turned and hurried away.

"You know just about everybody, don't you Vidalia?" Bobby asked.

She shrugged. "You live in the same town for as many years as I have, you get to know people."

"I lived in the same town for more than a decade, and didn't even know my next door neighbors."

"Well that's a shame," she said softly. "They might have been nice folks. And I know they missed out by not knowing you."

He lowered his head, but she saw the dimple dig into his cheek when he smiled. He had the most beautiful dimples. "I wish I was worthy of that praise, Vidalia," he muttered.

Age hadn't done him any harm, she thought, watching his face while he wasn't watching hers. She wished she could say the same for herself.

Her hair was still just as dark and curly and long as ever, but there was a gray strand here and there. She had laugh lines around her eyes, but she would never regret those. Her daughters had put those there, every last one of them, and she wouldn't trade the years raising her girls for a smooth-skinned face now. Her figure wasn't stick thin anymore. Never had been, but the curves were curvier than they used to be—she was well aware of that, she thought, looking down at her strong, denim clad thighs.

She glanced sideways at Bobby and found his eyes on her. They were sliding down her body, as far as the table between them would allow, even though she wore ordinary jeans and an unbuttoned long-sleeved western shirt over a snug fitting tank, which was her usual attire. She also wore boots. She had to head to the corral after this to open up for the evening, so she hadn't dressed up. Besides, she didn't want him to think she was trying to impress him.

Bobby said, "I've got a proposition for you, Vidalia."

She lifted her gaze from the menu she'd been pretending to peruse. "I'll just bet you do, Bobby Joe."

He smiled and waggled his eyebrows. "I never forgot, you know. That one night—"

Her menu fell to the table as if pushed from her hands by the breath that rushed out of her lungs. "That's not what you said at the time."

He waved a dismissive hand. "I mean the early part of it. When we danced all alone at the Corral and wound up making out like teenagers." He smiled wistfully. "The only part I forgot is the part after we drank a little more."

"A lot more," she corrected, as she felt the blood rush to her face and lowered her head. Her relief that his memory of that night hadn't returned was so huge she almost floated out of the chair. "I don't want to talk about that night, though."

"Why not? It was the greatest night of my life."

"It was the greatest sin of mine. My greatest shame."

He closed his eyes. "I've never stopped thinking about it."

"I've never stopped trying to forget it. And if that's what you came to talk about, then this lunch is over before it begins." She slapped the menu closed, laid it on the table, and made as if to rise, but he shot his hands out to cover hers, and she stopped.

"I won't bring it up again. I promise."

She looked into his eyes. Everything in her shivered with memory, with an old longing she'd thought had died. But it had only been lying dormant, and apparently, growing bigger all the time. And now it was awake and alive and more powerful than ever before. She banked it and, giving a nod, relaxed into her seat again. "I'm gonna hold you to that, Bobby."

"You won't have to. My word is my word."

"Good to know that hasn't changed." She heaved a sigh. "So back on topic, what's this...proposition you have for me?"

"Ah, that. Well now, I need your help."

"My help? With what?" She blinked across the table at him. "Not the saloon that you're building to put mine out of business?"

He nodded precisely twice. She shook her head side to side in time with his nod. Bridget cleared her throat. "Here are those drinks." She set a big mug of beer in front of Bobby and a china tea cup with a pink rose on the front and gold trim around the lip in front of Vidalia. "Do you know what you want to order yet?"

"You can't be serious," Vidalia said. Some distant part of her thought she should address the Haggerty girl, or at least postpone this discussion until she'd left again, but the words were flying free and she couldn't stop them. "Why would I *help* you with your saloon?"

"Because I helped you with yours," he said. Then he smiled his charming smile up at Bridget. "You have anything seasonal? I'm feeling festive."

Bridget smiled right back, though she was clearly feeling a little nervous about having arrived at the wrong moment. "The specials are all festive. Grandma Betty's idea of festive, anyway," she said, and she pointed to the list of daily specials inside the menu. "Reindeer Pot Roast, which as you can guess is venison based. Holiday Ham or Turkey and Trimmings. Full meals or sandwich plates, your call."

Vidalia was trying to drag her shocked eyes off Bobby Joe, but for the life of her, she couldn't.

Bridget said, "Take your time. I'll come back in a few minutes," and then she hurried away.

She had manners, that one did. Betty Jean had raised those girls right.

Vidalia was gaping, but Bobby Joe was giving her those same smitten puppy dog eyes he'd given her all those years ago."

"You owe me, Vidalia. I helped you get the OK Corral up and running."

"I paid you for that help."

"I worked for next to nothing."

She shrugged. "Hey, I didn't name your price, you did."

"And I named one so cheap you wouldn't be able to say no."

"Not my fault. You must've had your reasons."

"I did. I wanted to be around you as much as I could possibly manage."

She had no snappy comeback that time. Her words got stuck in her throat, and she sat there staring at him.

"Vidalia Brand, you knocked my socks off the first time I laid eyes on you. And I'll tell you what, lady. You still do."

She picked up his beer and drank it straight down. All in one draught. When she set it down again, she lowered her head and whispered, "I was a married woman, Bobby."

"Not legally," he said, sounding just like Maya. "But I know, I know you don't see it that way. And that's why I left after that night—"

"Will you keep it down?" She looked around the all but empty restaurant. "Jeeze, you think I want my greatest shame broadcast on the evening news?"

"Oh, come on Vidalia, no one cares about a one-night stand neither of us can remember."

"My daughters would care."

He went silent, staring deep into her eyes for a long silent moment, until she had to lower hers.

Bridget came back. Vidalia said, "We're both having the buffet, hon."

"Okay, sure. Um, just help yourselves when you're ready." She turned and walked away and Vidalia felt a little bit guilty for not being friendlier. But not nearly as guilty as she felt over what had happened all those years ago. Especially the parts she'd never told Bobby.

At least she hadn't lied to him. Outright. She had kept a pretty damned huge secret from him though.

"You know it's odd, how we both blacked out that night," he said. "I mean, I was drinking way too much at the time, that much I know. Being in love with another man's wife was a little more than I was man enough to deal with back then. But you never drank much. A little more than usual that night, but it didn't seem like enough that you'd forget."

"And this is coming from what? Your non-memory of anything that happened?"

"I remember a lot of it. I remember...most of it."

She remembered all of it. Including waking up in his arms the next morning in the storage room on a bed made of drop cloths and their respective coats.

"And yet you left town the very next day. Not a note. Not a goodbye." Not even after that long night of lovemaking, the likes of which Vidalia hadn't seen before or since. If she didn't burn in hell for it, then there was no justice in the world.

"What was left to say? You pretty much said it all when I woke up."

She had. She'd been mortified. Horrified at what she had done. Her husband had been out of town "on business" for two months at that point. She'd been working with Bobby for six. Together every day. All day. Working, bickering playfully, laughing, touching sometimes, always accidentally of course. *Feeling.*

She'd woke up naked, still wrapped in his arms. And she'd been disgusted with herself. Even though by then she was sure her husband was cheating on her. Johnny couldn't have gone two months without sex if he'd been in a coma. But that didn't make it right. She didn't know he had another wife, one he'd already been married to when he'd married her. And two kids, to boot.

So she'd got up, got dressed, and waited for Bobby to wake. And when he had, she'd said, "This was the biggest mistake of my life. I can't see you anymore, Bobby. Not ever."

She remembered how hurt he'd seemed and how he'd tried to apologize, saying he didn't even remember coming into the store room, much less what had happened afterward. And she'd said she didn't remember either. But she did. Oh, how vividly she did.

And then she'd walked out and gone home before her four little girls ever woke up. The sitter had fallen asleep on the sofa and never knew what time Vidalia had come home. No one did. No one besides her had any clue what had happened.

Bobby reached across the table and covered her hand with his. "You're not married anymore, Vidalia."

"God, Bobby, a whole lifetime has passed between then and now. You can't just come back here and expect all those old feelings between us to be the same."

"I didn't. I didn't expect that. Not at all. I just..." He sighed heavily. "You know why I left, Vidalia?"

She shook her head slowly. He caught her chin with his fingertip and turned it toward him. She could've closed her eyes, but that would've been cowardly, and Vidalia Brand was no coward. So she stared into his eyes and knew she'd compounded her sins by lying to him just now. All those old feelings were exactly the same, just buried under years and years of guilt and shame.

"I left because I knew that if I stayed, I was going to have you," he said, his voice as rough as if he'd gargled with broken glass. "I wouldn't have let up until you gave in to me, and you would have because you felt the same way I did. I know you did. But I also knew you'd never forgive yourself if that happened. I knew it would tear you apart. Just like leaving you tore me apart. I chose to take the pain rather than give it to you. But now...."

His voice trailed off there, and lowering his head, he shook it slowly, then pushed one hand back through his hair. He let go of her hands and leaned back in his chair. "Damn, this is not the conversation I intended to have here today."

"I should hope not."

"I'm sorry," he said. "I'm not here to seduce you back into my arms. I'm not." Oddly, it sounded almost as if he was trying to convince himself more than her. "I'm just here to open The Long Branch. Opening night, I'm gonna dress as Marshall Matt Dillon. You know, the vest, the badge, the gun belt. And I need a Miss Kitty to be my hostess for the evening."

She closed her eyes slowly. She had lied to this man for more than two decades. Okay, omitted the truth. The dishonesty shamed her straight to the roots of her hair, almost as much as that night she'd spent in his arms.

And now, to know that he'd left town to spare her having to say no to him. To spare her the guilt of eventually saying yes.

She'd sworn off drinking that night, but it didn't change the truth of the lie she'd told. Or of the other much bigger secret she'd kept for all these years. The one he really *did* deserve to know.

She lowered her head to hide the tears that were springing into her eyes. "I dressed as Miss Kitty last Halloween at the Corral," she said.

"I know. I saw a picture in the local paper. That's what gave me the idea for the Long Branch, to tell you the truth."

She closed her eyes, thought she was going to regret her next words, but she owed this man even more than he knew. "All right. I'll help you."

"You will?" He seemed both stunned and delighted. "You will, you'll do it?"

"I'll do it. You're right. I owe you. I can have one of the girls handle the Corral that night. Or just close it for the evening. What night are you opening?"

"The twenty-second."

She lifted her eyebrows. "It's not the twenty-first, so Selene might be free."

He frowned. "She has plans on the twenty-first?"

"Winter Solstice," Vidalia said. "She's into...." She gave up, waved both hands in a never mind gesture. "She's always been different from the other girls."

"She's the only one I never met," he said.

"Oh, you'll be meeting her. And seeing the rest of them again, too. Those girls of mine are way too interested in what I've been doing in my private time since you blew back into town."

"I am looking forward to it," he said. And he cupped her hands in his, pulled them to his lips, and kissed her knuckles. "Thank you, Vidalia. I mean it. Thank you."

"You're welcome," she told him, and she didn't try to suppress the delicious shiver caused by the touch of his lips on her skin. Again. Finally.

CHAPTER FOUR

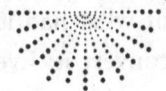

$\mathcal{H}$e didn't want to say goodbye when their lunch date ended, so he was glad when an aging woman who introduced herself as Betty Haggerty came out from the kitchen, wiping her hands on her apron, and smiling at Vidalia. He was introduced briefly, before the older woman tugged his date away to engage her in what looked to be an important conversation. He watched them, because he couldn't take his eyes off his raven-haired beauty.

Vidalia was as sexy as ever. She'd come in work clothes, probably because she'd rather be shot between those pretty eyes of hers than to let him think she'd dressed up for his sake. But he kind of thought she had. Her hair was down, not bundled up behind her head like it had been at the Corral the other night. The jeans were snug and hugged her in all the right places, and watching her walk across the restaurant to the buffet had been so delicious an experience that he made sure to let her head back to the table first, so he could watch her all over again. Her hair was just as jet black as ever, springy curls falling way past her shoulders, and her eyes were just as brown.

He'd never got over her. He'd been sure from day one, she was the only woman he would ever love.

But he couldn't have her, and that was that. And so he'd tried to move on. He'd met Judith, married her, raised a family with her, and thanked his lucky stars for the three sons she'd given him. But Vidalia had remained in his heart the entire time.

He hadn't told the boys about...any of this. Not that he was coming here, or why. Not what had led up to the decision to buy the feed store and convert it. Even though it was all for them. Telling them now would ruin the surprise later. And he certainly hadn't told them about his condition, which would ruin his last holiday season ever, and his plan to make it the most memorable of his life.

He didn't want to think about that now, anyway. He wanted to throw himself into The Long Branch, because that was what he loved doing best. And he wanted to throw himself into spending time with Vidalia, because, though he'd never been a saint, he believed that he deserved as much pleasure as he could muster from what was left of his life. And whether he deserved it or not, which was, he supposed, not up to him to judge, he was damn well going to take it.

He was a little hurt that Vidalia didn't seem to be harboring the same endless adoration for him that he had for her. But he was also glad she didn't return his feelings. It wouldn't be fair to encourage that and would end up breaking her heart later on. But since she was so immune to his charms, he figured it was safe for him to spend time with her.

It would be just like getting the Corral up and running together. Just like old times.

After a few minutes, her conversation with Betty Haggerty, who seemed a bit too old to be running an entire restaurant, wound down. The older woman, he noticed, looked tired, and that made him take another look around the place, and wonder whether it was just empty because it was midday, or whether it was in trouble. And as he examined the place with new eyes, he noticed things. The fresh coat of paint that was long overdue, the crack in one of the out of the way windows, trying to hide behind curtains that were starting to lose their vibrance and fray a bit at the edges.

Haggerty House, he thought, might just be in trouble.

But Vidalia didn't mention a word about that as they went their separate ways. No, she wouldn't, would she? Vidalia Brand was a woman who could keep a confidence. Trustworthy. He'd always trusted her. She'd rather be shot than lie, or betray someone she cared about.

In the parking lot, he walked her to her truck, then stood there like a sixteen year old, wondering if he should go in for a goodbye kiss.

She shot the thought down when she leaned up and planted one on his cheek. Not at all what he'd had in mind. "I'll see you soon, Bobby Joe. And I'll dig out my Miss Kitty costume before I do."

"You don't have to. I got you a brand new one." At auction, for a small fortune, because it had been one of several actually worn by Amanda Blake in the TV series. She'd been five six, a good four inches taller than Vidalia. But a full foot plus shorter than her co-star, James Arness. He'd landed an original Matt Dillon costume worn by the six-foot seven actor. He was only six two. But he'd had both costumes altered, and the height difference between him and Vidalia would look very close to that between Marshall Dillon and his own Miss Kitty. A foot.

One foot was, he thought, the perfect height difference, as he looked down at her, and she looked up at him. Her eyelids lowered as the color rose in those perfect apple cheeks of hers, and she said, "I'd better go. Gotta open soon."

"Okay. Thanks for this, Vidalia. And for helping out with the Long Branch."

"*De nada*," she said, and then crushed his heart by turning and getting into her truck. She did flash him a bright smile, though, as she drove away. And yet he thought something was bothering her. There were shadows behind her eyes.

~

Later that afternoon, Bobby stood in his all but finished saloon, looking around the place and planning their grand entrance. He might have Vidalia come down the curving staircase in the red and gold Miss Kitty getup with her curls all bundled up high on her head and a fake beauty mark on her cheek. He'd be waiting at the bottom in his Matt Dillon getup. That was where the boys came in to play their parts in the skit he had planned for opening night. Of course he had yet to tell them, and the skit was only in his head right now, but he would be doing that later today.

Absently, he opened a cardboard box of the glossy flyers that had been delivered while he'd been out. They'd been waiting by the front door, under the tarp, when he'd come back. They had come out beautifully

Citizens of Big Falls, celebrate the Holidays in the Old West. Come to the Long Branch for our opening night, December 23rd. Have a great meal, see a show, absolutely free of charge. Merry Christmas, Neighbors.

Your friend,

Bobby Joe McIntyre

He smiled when he eyed the line drawings of him as Matt Dillon and Vidalia as Miss Kitty. Feeling confident she would say yes, he'd hired an artist who'd used a photo of Vidalia in her Miss Kitty getup. Bobby had found it on one of her daughters' Facebook pages. It had come out great. Not as great as she was in person, of course, but great, all the same.

As he stood there looking at the flyers, he heard the front door swing slowly open and looked up to see his oldest son,

Jason, across the room. It never failed to amaze him, looking at his sons. Grown, strapping young men, as different from each other as they were from him. Jason was six four, and his upper body showed his penchant for workouts. He was the silent one, the brooder who never showed his feelings. But he was wearing his heart on his sleeve just then, looking at his father in a way that left no doubt in Bobby's mind that Jason knew. He held his son's eyes and tried to think of anything else that would've caused those tears he saw swimming in them, but there wasn't anything else.

Jason looked away, tried to hide his emotions, swept the place with his gaze, gave a nod of approval. "So this is the secret project no one wanted to tell me about."

"I just sent you an email. All three of you. Wanted to get you down here for the grand opening."

Jason couldn't seem to meet his father's eyes. His own were everywhere but there, in fact. "Since when do you stay for the grand opening? Isn't that the new owner's job?"

"Usually." Bobby went around behind the bar, took down a mug. "Pull up a stool, son, and I'll pour you a beer."

"I talked to Mom," Jason said as he crossed the room, took a seat on one of the tall barstools. The saddle-shaped seats were made of leather and suede. Ladies could hang their handbags from the pommels. Bobby thought it was ingenious, himself.

"How *is* Judith these days? She happy with old what's-his-name?"

"It's Stu and you know it. And yes, she's happy." Jason sighed, lowered his head and shook it slowly. "She told me about...your condition."

"She shouldn't have done that." He said it softly, because he didn't know what else to say. His gut wanted to reassure his son that it wasn't all that serious, that everything would be fine, but it wouldn't. He was on a waiting list for a bone marrow donor that would stop the blood disease from killing him if he got it before the symptoms set in. From that point, which could be any day now, it would move fast. They'd be out of time. And his shot of finding a donor in time were slim to none. He had an odd blood type, one his sons had no inherited.

"Why the hell not?" Jason asked. "Don't you think I have a right to know that my father is...is dying?"

"It's my news to tell, son." He slid a hand over Jason's on the bar. "And I wanted to choose when and how to break it to the three of you." He sighed, then shot Jason a look. "Have you told your brothers?"

"Not yet."

"Why not?"

Jason sighed, shook his head sadly. "Didn't want to go off half-cocked. Thought I should talk to you first. And besides, it's almost Christmas."

"Our last one together," Bobby said softly. "We think alike, you and me. I didn't want to ruin everyone's holiday with this news, either. I wanted to make this Christmas special, the best one yet. And I didn't want it spoiled by premature grieving, son. Hell, you'll have time enough to mourn me after I'm gone. Don't start early, all right?"

Jason stared at his dad for a long time. Then he said, "What is it, exactly?"

He shrugged. "It's a blood disease. Bone marrow's not producing the right cells or something. There are lots of long-winded explanations but what it comes down to is that it'll be fast once it kicks in. I'm not gonna suffer."

"But they do bone marrow transplants, right? Couldn't one of us—"

"My doc looked into all that. Yes, a transplant could cure it. No, none of you boys are compatible, and yes, I am on a waiting list for a donor. If one comes along in time, this conversation will be moot." He shifted his gaze away, feeling guilty for throwing even that morsel of false hope his son's way.

"How long...do you have?"

He shrugged. "Doc said three months at the outside."

"And how long ago was that?"

Bobby bit his lip, took a deep breath, nodded hard. "'Bout three months."

The bar was between them. Bobby didn't know if Jason would've hugged him or not. Probably not. He wasn't a hugging sort of a man.

Instead, he just kept his head down as he took a bracing gulp of his beer. "You didn't want to spend that time with us?"

"I had something I had to do first."

"Right. Sell off damn near everything you owned, buy a feed store in some backwoods part of Oklahoma, and turn it into a saloon. It's always been work first with you. Even now." He picked up one of the flyers, eyed it with disdain, and dropped it again.

Bobby withstood the accusation without flinching. It hurt, but he had it coming. "You're right about that last part. It always *has been* work first with me. It's something I regret right to my bones, son, I'll tell you that. Sometimes it takes facing his own mortality to wake a man up to what really matters. But I am awake now. And you're dead wrong on the rest of it."

"Then why are you here? Why didn't you come to us, talk to us?"

Bobby Joe drew a deep breath, counted to five, let it out again. "There are guest rooms upstairs. Just like in the real Long Branch. Here." He pulled an old fashioned, heavy key on a numbered wooden ring out from underneath the bar, and slid it across to him. "Go on up. Take your beer with you. They hooked up the wireless yesterday, so you can get online all right. Get your email."

"I didn't bring anything. I didn't plan to stay. I just wanted...."

He shook his head. "Hell, I don't know what I wanted."

"You can get what you need in town. Your brothers'll be here by tomorrow. I hope. You might as well wait for them to get here at least." He shook a finger at his son. "But don't you tell them about the...about my condition. It can wait. Consider it my final request, if that's what it takes, but I'm serious about this Jason. After Christmas, not one minute before December twenty-sixth. All right?"

Jason met his father's eyes, pressed his lips. "I don't know if they'll ever forgive me if I do that."

"Then I guess you've gotta decide the right thing to do. Go on up, son."

The daughters of Vidalia Brand didn't work full time at the OK Corral anymore. Two of them were mothers, and all five were married with careers and lives of their own. Hanging out in the family saloon wasn't really necessary, though they did still come by anytime she needed an extra hand. If a barmaid or waitress got sick or she needed extra help for busy nights, the summer holidays and Halloween. New Year's Eve they usually needed the whole crew, sons in law included. But on Christmas Eve, the Corral was always closed. Family was what mattered on Christmas.

Tonight wasn't one of those busy nights at all, so Vidalia was kind of surprised to see Maya, her firstborn, and Melusine, her fourth, come in through the batwing doors at about 6:30 pm. The place was all but empty. One or two regulars nursing their beers slowly in opposite corners, too bored with life to wait for things to pick up. Always the first to arrive and the last to leave, usually with some friend helping them home.

So it was good and quiet, and the girls knew that it was at this time of the evenin', so she expected they had something on their minds. Something discussion-worthy, and she had a pretty good idea its name was RJR McIntyre.

And she was right. When they came up to the bar, it was Maya who slid a glossy poster across the hardwood and said, "Have you seen this?"

"Course she's seen it," Mel said. "She's *in* it."

"What's this now?" Vidalia came to the bar, wiping her hands on her apron, and picked up the flyer. Then she smiled. "Dang, he was sure confident I'd say yes, wasn't he? I don't know whether to be amused or ticked off."

"Say yes to *what*?" Mel demanded.

Vidalia lifted her gaze, narrowed it, and gave each of the girls a long, steady look. They knew enough to stay silent in the wake of that look, too. "I'll thank you to take that tone out of your voice, young lady. I'm still your mother, and not only that, I'm fairly certain I could still whip your ass, should the situation call for it."

Maya blinked in shock, then turned her head slightly, probably to hide a smile. She was a mother now, too. She got this sort of thing.

"Have a seat. I'll pour us all some coffee, and we can talk like human beings."

"Mama, you can't possibly trust this guy who just showed up out of the blue and plans to open a competing–"

Vidalia pointed at a table, then turned to head into the kitchen behind the bar. The short order cook showed up at eight. Until then, the crowds were light enough that she could handle any cooking needed on her own.

She filled three mugs, fixed them all, knowing her daughters' coffee fixin's by heart, and carried them out to the table in two hands. The girls were sitting, waiting, and speaking to each other in urgent, hushed tones that silenced the second she returned.

Vidalia sat down. "So, I had lunch with Bobby Joe McIntyre today, and he asked me to play hostess for him on his opening night. Since I owe the man more than I can ever hope to repay, I said I would. The Corral will be closed on the 23rd in a show of support and friendship with the Long Branch. Objections should be put in writing, and filed in the trash can. I don't answer to anyone these days and haven't in twenty years, in case that's slipped your minds." She sipped her coffee and pulled the flyer closer, eyeing it and smiling. "It's very flattering, don't you think?"

"Mama," Mel said, "Alex and I did a little poking around–"

Vidalia looked across the table at her daughter. "Alex and you did what, now?"

"Okay, Alex refused. I did it myself."

"Did what yourself, daughter?"

"Don't be mad."

She'd come in here all bluff and bluster and now she was realizing just how far she had overstepped.

"I asked her to, Mom," Maya said. "I'm worried about you."

"So I checked into RJR McIntyre's recent activities. The man's net worth is in the billions. Most of it's invested, but just recently he sold off almost everything. Converted it into cash and bought gold with every bit of it."

Vidalia frowned. "What a billionaire does with his assets is kind of his own business, don't you think, Mel?"

"Ma, when rich men start converting assets to cash and squirreling it away, it usually means they're expecting to be prosecuted for something."

"Oh, does it now?"

"I've never seen one that didn't," she said.

"Huh. Well, I'll take that under advisement, Melusine. But it really doesn't have anything to do with me, and even less to do with you. I'll add that it doesn't change my decision to help him open his saloon next week."

"But Mom–"

"No more snooping, Melusine. That's out of line and the both of you are old enough to know it."

Melusine looked at her sister. Maya shrugged. "It's only because we care about you Mom."

"I accept that's what it seems like from your perspective," Vidalia said. "Would you like to know what it feels like from my end?" She didn't wait for them to answer before telling them. "It feels like you don't think I'm smart enough to make my own decisions. Like you don't have any respect for the wisdom I've gained, raising five girls and starting a business almost single-handedly. Like you think that when a woman hits fifty-some-thing, she turns into a blithering idiot who needs a caretaker."

The girls looked more horrified with every word she spoke, and she knew she had finally got through to them.

"We don't think that at all, Mom," Maya said. "I don't ever want you to think we do."

"Same here," Mel put in. But for some reason it didn't carry the same conviction. "I don't think you're an idiot. I just think when romance is involved, even the smartest woman can make a mistake."

"If there *were* romance involved, it would be my mistake to make. Not yours." Vidalia pushed away from the table and stood up. "This conversation is over. I've got a business to run. You girls have a good night."

Sighing, they got up, too. Mel reached for the glossy flyer on the table, but Vidalia grabbed it first. "I'll just keep this. Night, girls."

Vidalia had no idea what kind of demon possessed her, but after closing time, she found herself once again, parked outside the Long Branch. This time, though, she pulled right on into the parking lot and sat there in plain sight, staring at the impressive face of the place.

The concealing tent had vanished sometime during the day

today, and she'd spotted those glossy posters hanging on telephone poles and sign posts all the way here.

Bobby had done a great job. The front entrance had four glossy log pillars that supported a huge sign that read Long Branch Saloon. The lettering managed to be both rustic and fancy at the same time. Rustic, because it looked as if it had been burned into the wood with a cattle brand. Fancy, because the first letter of each word was kind of swirly.

It looked great. And with those signs all over town, she figured there was no longer any point in hiding what was going on beneath the tarp. Still, she'd expected more. Maybe a little fanfare, the high school marching band, the town supervisor—Big Falls was too small for a mayor—and a ribbon cutting ceremony. Something like that.

No one was awake in there. The place was dark, and she was sitting here like some kind of midnight creeper, spying on a long ago lover and wondering if he really believed that nothing had happened between them that night. Or if he had come back here to find out the truth, once and for all. The secret she'd been keeping all these years.

A secret she'd never had any right to keep.

A light came on inside just as she decided to drive quietly away. The front door opened. No point hiding now. She opened her door and got out of the pickup, landing light and easy on the ground as he came toward her. But when she got the courage to look up, it wasn't Bobby Joe's eyes she found blinking at her. Similar ones, for sure, but not his.

"You're her," he said. "You're Vidalia Brand."

She blinked in surprise. "Well, I sure was last I checked. How do you know?"

He lowered his head, nodding slow. "My father's...mentioned your name once or twice. And then of course, there's the poster."

"You're one of Bobby's boys?" she asked, because it wasn't

right, the rush of pleasure coursing through her at knowing Bobby Joe had spoken of her...once or twice. "I'd have guessed that in another second or two. You've got those same blue eyes."

"Jason," he said, extending a big hand. "Pleased to meet you, Ms. Brand."

"You can call me Vidalia," she said. "I had no idea you were in town."

"I only just arrived. Dad didn't tell me...any of us...what he was up to. At least, not until I'd already tracked him down on my own."

Something was wrong with the young man. He looked downright troubled.

"My brothers will be here tomorrow," he said. "Dad sent an email after I left asking us all to be here for the grand opening. I think we're supposed to play outlaws or something."

She smiled. "You've gotta admit, he's very good at this," she said, looking at the saloon.

"Is that why you're here in the middle of the night?" he asked. "To get a look at it, now that it's uncovered?"

She didn't say yes or no. "I own the OK Corral, other end of town. We only just closed for the night, or I wouldn't be creeping around in the wee hours."

"Dad's not here," he said.

She nodded. "That's okay. I didn't expect he'd be up at this hour, even if he was...." Then she frowned. "Where on earth can he be at this hour?"

"Said he couldn't sleep. Wanted to go see the falls this town is named after. Said he hadn't been out there since he'd been back."

She nodded slow, but she was starting to get a little worried feeling running up her spine. "Does he normally summon all his sons to an opening of a new saloon?"

"Never. But then again, he usually resells them before they open, turning a healthy profit in the process."

She tipped her head to one side. "Why do you think this time is different?"

He looked her right in the eyes, opened his mouth like he was about to say something, then closed it again and looked past her at the sky. "You'd have to ask him that, ma'am."

"All right, I will." Was that a tear glimmering in Jason McIntyre's eye? What in the hay was going on with this clan? "It was nice meeting you, Jason. Once your brothers arrive, I'd like to have you all over for a meal."

"Why?" he asked. Flat out, blunt, no bull with this one.

She shrugged. "Well, if your family is gonna run a saloon in this town, I figure I can either make you my enemies or make you my friends. I've got enough enemies, so...." she shrugged.

He relaxed, maybe let his guard down even, and smiled at her. "You're every bit as pretty as my dad always said, Ms. Brand."

"Vidalia," she reminded him. "And thank you. Goodnight, Jason." She turned back toward her truck, then stopped and faced him once more. "Whatever's troubling you, you know, things have a way of working out."

"Not this time," he said softly. He lowered his head, shook it, and turning, walked back into the saloon, leaving her there alone.

Vidalia got into her truck and didn't even try to talk herself out of driving to the Falls. It was an argument she'd have lost anyway.

～

Bobby Joe found himself a perfect spot in the little clearing that faced the falls, pulled up a log for a stool, and sat himself down. He had never been one to spend a lot of time mulling on spiritual matters. But learning that you only had a short time to live probably changed that in everyone. Even the most hardened of hearts, he imagined.

Now, though, as he sat there watching that waterfall flowing like it would never stop, it hit him that it would. Eventually, it would stop. The water would dry up or the cliff would erode back far enough to make it level with the rest of the riverbed, and there would be no more waterfall.

He was going to stop, too. And he wondered if there would be any more Bobby Joe once he crossed that great divide. What was on the other side? Was there an other side? How could you go on without a body, and what would that be like? Did he truly believe there was anything after death?

He'd never given these things a lot of thought. Considered himself a good man, a decent man. He didn't think he'd done anything worthy of hellfire, if there was such a thing. But he wasn't sure he'd done anything worthy of heaven, either.

He'd never felt the call to pray before. But as he sat there on that log, in the cold night air, watching his breath form clouds in the darkness, he thought maybe it was time. He looked up at the stars, and he said whatever came to mind. Didn't think first, just opened his mouth. And the words that came out were these. "I don't know what I'm supposed to do here, God. I mean, I know what I *want* to do. Spend time here, in the place where I spent the days that turned out to be my happiest, though I didn't know that at the time. That's probably a life lesson right there, isn't it, God? Anytime you're laughing, smiling, happy, might just turn out to be your happiest moment ever. Probably a good thing to tell young folks. Too late for it to do me much good, I guess. Still, I wanted to come back here, to where I was happiest, and spend time with the woman I was happiest with, the one I could never have for my own. I wanted to spend my last Christmas here, with her, and with my boys, because it seems like it's something they should experience. Something they should know if they hope to know me—really know me, deep down. They have to know what made me happy. So here I am, doing what I want to do with the little bit of time I have left, and while I know I'm late in asking, I figure better late than never. What do *you* want me to spend my final days doing? Cause if you tell me, Lord, I'll give it my best shot. I promise, I will."

He sat there a while, not expecting an answer, exactly. Maybe a sign or a flash of insight or something like that. But the only thing that came was the sound of a pickup truck and the brief gleam of its bouncing headlights as it came to a stop near where he'd left his own. A door slammed, and then he heard footsteps in the tall, dead winter grasses and weeds, and knew someone was coming toward him.

And he also knew before she got all the way there, who it was. Vidalia. He smelled her signature scent–the same one she'd worn all those years before. It used to drive him crazy, make him want to bury his head near her neck and rub himself in it.

She didn't say a word, just came right on out and plunked herself down on the log next to him. "Beautiful night for star gazing," she said.

"Sure is," he agreed, and as he looked up at the stars, he sent God a smile. *Message received. Thanks.*

"Cold though," she went on.

"Downright brisk."

"I met your son, Jason, tonight," she said.

He looked at her then, figuring he'd pretended the stars held more interest for long enough. And then he just drank in the sight of her. She wore a suede jacket that ended at the waist just above her jeans. And those boots of hers with heels most women her age wouldn't even try to run around in. Her hair was long and wild and dancing with the chilly breeze that the falls seemed to generate all on their own.

"He seems like a good man. You raised him well."

"His mother did," Bobby Joe admitted. "I was too busy with work to take much credit for the man he turned out to be."

"Well, it's never too late to start. Seems like you know that, already. Is that why you summoned them all out here for the grand opening?"

"He told you about that, did he?" She nodded. "He tell you anything else?"

She smiled a little, lowered her eyes. "That you talked about me. Said I was pretty."

"Nothing but the truth," he said.

"He seemed...I don't know. Sad. Troubled."

Bobby looked away from her probing eyes. "I hope that changes when I give him his Christmas present."

"Oh? You have a great one in mind?"

He nodded. "Best one ever. The Long Branch. I'm signing it over to him and his brothers before we open."

She lifted her brows in surprise. "But Bobby Joe, I thought you were planning to run it yourself." Then she looked at her hands in her lap. "Does that mean you're...not planning to stay here in Big Falls?"

"You say that as if you care. Do you, Vidalia?"

She didn't look up and she didn't answer. So he caught her chin with his forefinger and tipped her head up, and he was surprised to see tears sparkling on her thick lashes.

And what happened next, well, he didn't have much control over that at all. Because if he had, it wouldn't have happened. He looked at her for about a second longer, and then he kissed her.

Her arms crept round his neck, and his slid around her waist, and she kissed him right back, and that made him want to kiss her even more, which resulted in her kissing him back even more. They sat there on that fallen log, all wrapped up in each other, making out like a couple of horny teenagers. And when he lifted his head and stared into her beautiful dark eyes, there was snow falling on her hair. Tiny white flakes of it drifted down all around them. It wouldn't stick. And come morning, no one would even know it had ever happened.

It was like a gift, just for the two of them.

She smiled up at him. "I've been praying for snow," she said softly.

"Are your prayers always answered, Vidalia?" he asked. He wondered if, in her experience, God answered her prayers as quickly as He had just answered Bobby's own. He'd asked what he should be doing with the time he had left, and God had sent him Vidalia. He'd as much as told him to go ahead and spend his final days with her, just the way he wanted to.

Made him wish he'd talked to the Big Guy more often. He hadn't expected it to be that easy or for the answer to be that immediate, that clear. Unless it was just his imagination, and coincidence, and wishful thinking.

She was nodding hard. "Always, Bobby Joe. Every single time I pray, I get an answer. Every once in a while, though, the answer is no."

He nodded at her. "So you're still a believer?"

"Look around us," she said turning her head and looking at the stars, the waterfall crashing down, and the gentle fall of snowflakes in the dark. "How can I not be?"

His heart knotted up and told him right then that he was as much in love with this woman as he had ever been. And he knew it wasn't fair not to tell her the truth, not when it seemed like she might be feeling fondly toward him as well.

But not yet, not tonight. Tonight was too special, too magical to ruin with talk about death and dying.

He slid his arm around her shoulders, held her near to his side, and continued looking at the sky and noticing how you could hardly tell the stars from the snowflakes, way up high. "I need to get a Christmas tree for the Long Branch," he said.

"Well, I need to get one for the Corral," she told him. "What do you say we do it together?"

"I say, you bet. How about tomorrow?"

"Tomorrow's great. Perfect, in fact. It's Sunday, so it'll have to be in the afternoon. I go to church in the morning." She took a deep breath, lowered her eyes. "You could come with me, if you want."

He was quiet for a long moment. "I um...God and I are working through some issues right now, Vidalia. We're communicating, Him and I. But I'm not quite ready to visit Him at home just yet.

She frowned and studied his face through the snowflakes, but he didn't elaborate.

CHAPTER FIVE

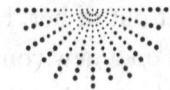

*V*idalia was like a kid on Christmas Eve for the rest of that night. She didn't drive home, she floated on a cloud of romantic pink fluff she hadn't felt since....

Well, heck, since Bobby Joe had left town so long ago.

She felt as giddy as a seventeen-year-old in love for the first time. And maybe that was unseemly and maybe it was silly, but it was. That's all. It just was.

She got herself home and took a long hot shower and didn't sleep a wink all night. Just laid there, imagining how it would be if she and Bobby could start over. Imagining how it would be if he stuck around Big Falls, and what people would think about that. And yet all that time, there was a dark shadow lurking in the back of her mind, casting a pall over her excited, romantic thoughts. The secret she'd kept from him. The one that was standing smack in between the two of them. But she pushed that shadow out of her mind and kept it at bay, just like she'd done for the past twenty-plus years.

She was up before dawn, bustling around the kitchen to get Sunday dinner underway. It was a family tradition. Even on Sundays when the girls and their families didn't come to church, they always came to Sunday dinner. And while she didn't want to get ahead of herself here, she was thinking of inviting Bobby Joe and his sons too, if they felt like coming along.

She was halfway through chopping onions to go into her famous pot roast, when the shadow of her guilt escaped from where she'd buried it, jumped up and hit her square in the chest, knocking the breath right out of her. Here she was, acting like she was about to embark on a new romance. But it wasn't new at all, was it? It was an old attraction that had led to the biggest sin she'd ever committed, which she had then compounded by adding the biggest lie she'd ever told.

She had no business feeling giddy or romantic or excited at all. And if anything was going to develop between her and Bobby Joe McIntyre, she had to take care of all of that old baggage first.

Because chances were, once he knew the truth, he'd never forgive her.

She should've told him long ago. It was the only stain on her soul, and it was a big one.

"Mom?" Selene had come in all but silently. "Are you crying?"

"Now what on earth would I have to cry about, darlin'? It's the onions, that's all." She used the blade of her knife to scrape them from the cutting board into the roasting pan, popped on the lid, and slid it into the oven to cook slowly. Then she went to the sink and washed her hands.

"You sure?" Selene asked.

"Sure I'm sure." Vidalia turned around to face her youngest daughter, and found herself lost in Selene's mysterious, pale blue eyes. "I don't suppose you're coming to church with me this morning," she asked to change the subject.

"Nope, not today. I celebrated the winter solstice last night, a couple of nights early, with some friends. It was more spiritual to me outside under the stars than church will ever be. It snowed, you know."

"I know! I saw it too. And I have to say, daughter, I agree with you there. It was truly magical, wasn't it?"

Selene frowned at her. "Now what were you doing up at three a.m., Mom?"

Vidalia shrugged and smiled mysteriously. "If you're not going to church, what are you doing here so early?"

"We thought we'd start putting up the Christmas lights on the house for you. You're late getting them out this year, and I can't stand looking at this place unlit this close to the holiday."

"We?" Vidalia asked.

Selene nodded. "Cory's outside unloading the ladder and tools."

"You're a good girl, Selene. To tell you the truth, I was hoping one of you would offer."

"You should've just asked."

She shrugged. "So, as long as you're here, will you keep an eye on my pot roast?"

"Sure thing, as long as you can tell me precisely what time to turn it off."

"I set a timer."

Selene smiled. "Go on to church. We'll have your halls decked in no time."

"Thank you, sweetie. And happy Winter Solstice."

Selene nodded. "Thank you."

"What's important to my girls is important to me." Vidalia took off her apron and headed out, sad that none of the snow from the night before had stuck. She'd forgot it was the twentieth already. Only two more nights until The Long Branch's grand opening. And only four more until Christmas Eve.

Where had the time gone?

~

The Reverend Jackson's sermon was about redemption. The son of God paying the price of our sins so we would never have to suffer death. It was a rouser, and one he repeated every year at Christmas and Easter, with minor tweaks.

Vidalia hung back afterward, chatting with her neighbors and friends, and wishing them happy holidays, until the last of them had left, and she stood there in the open, welcoming doors of the little country church all alone with the minister.

"I can see something's on your mind. You were preoccupied throughout my entire sermon," he said when the building was empty.

"Nonsense, I heard every single word."

He lifted his bushy, gray eyebrows as if he didn't quite believe that, but graciously didn't say so out loud. "Shall we go back inside for this, Vidalia?"

"I think we probably should, Reverend Jackson."

She went fist. He closed the red double doors and followed her down the aisle, around the pulpit, and through a small door into his little office in the back. Once there, he waved her into a chair while he poured coffee from a fairly fresh pot and handed her a cup. "It's decaf. At our age—"

"Speak for yourself," she said.

He sent her a wink. But his smile died as he settled into his chair behind the desk. "I can see you've got something on your mind, Vidalia."

She sighed. "I've committed a terrible sin, Reverend Jackson. And I just can't seem to figure out how to make it right, or if I even can.

"You?" he frowned. "Tongues have been wagging around town. About you and this McIntyre fellow. Bobby Joe. Does this have to do with him?"

She nodded. "Has to do with him, and me, and John...and maybe Selene. It's a guilty secret I've been keeping for more than two decades. I need you to tell me what to do."

He leaned back in his chair, steepled his fingers, was quiet for a long moment. Then he said, "We're not Catholics. You don't have to confess your sins to me."

"I know that. And if there was a way to figure this out without telling you, believe me, I'd rather. But I need guidance right now."

"Guidance." Reverend Jackson lowered his head, shaking it slowly. "I've learned more from you, Vidalia Brand, than you probably ever have or ever will from me. How to be a better parent to my daughter tops the list. So I'm

gonna give you a suggestion. And then if you feel you still need my guidance, I'm here to listen. All right?"

"All right."

"Whatever this is, whatever sin you committed, and whatever action you need to take to make it right, I want you to imagine one of your girls coming to you and pouring out everything that you were about to pour out to me. Every detail. Pretend it all happened to Maya or Edie or Kara. And then I want you to think about what you would tell them to do about it. How you would tell them to make it right."

She frowned at him. "It's not the same thing."

"It's exactly the same thing. They're the age you were when all this happened, aren't they?"

"Well, yes, but—"

"And you've raised them with the same moral code you believe in, haven't you?"

"Well of course I have but—"

"Write it all down, in the form of a letter to your younger self, or do it all inside your head, and talk to that younger Vidalia as if she were one of your own daughters. And then, Vidalia, no matter how hard, you take your own advice."

She sat there blinking slowly, and realizing that she knew exactly what she would tell one of her daughters about something like this. Tell the truth. Apologize profusely, beg forgiveness, offer atonement if necessary but first, buck up and tell the truth.

She drew a deep breath, got up from her seat and nodded. "You're one hell of a preacher, Reverend Jackson. I ever tell you that?"

"A time or two." He got up as well, reached out and took her hand, holding it between both of his own. "You remember one thing, Vidalia. God would never judge you as harshly as you are judging yourself right now. And there is nothing He wouldn't forgive."

She knew that. She knew all of that. Why had she been half-expecting divine retribution to come crashing down on her instead of loving forgiveness? She knew better, didn't she?

She just had to come clean. And not just to Bobby Joe. But to her daughters. Oh Lord, why couldn't doing the right thing ever be easy?

~

By noon, Bobby's sons had all arrived, and he'd given them the grand tour of the Long Branch, and pitched his invitation to help him with the grand opening, and then stick around for the holidays.

Joey was eager right off the bat, always up for a good time. Rob was less than enthusiastic, until Jason chimed in with an unrestrained yes and a meaningful look at the other two.

Hell, if they didn't already suspect something was up, they would now, Bobby Joe thought. But he wasn't going to let that put a damper on his day. He had every intention of enjoying his time with Vidalia this afternoon. So he left his sons with a list of jobs that needed doing around the place. Now that the crews of workers had packed up and gone home, there was no one to do it but him, and he tired a lot easier than he used to. Which was one of the symptoms that was supposed to warn him when things were...winding down. But he wasn't going to think about that right then.

He met Vidalia at the Christmas Tree farm five miles from Big Falls and drank in the sight of her in her snug jeans and suede jacket. She didn't wear a hat. It was chilly today, and he thought she should have but didn't say so. He'd brought along a hand saw, and the two of them hiked out into acres of pine trees with a map showing the layout of the place. Balsam firs this way, blue spruce that way, and so on.

"I'm dying for the perfect Douglas Fir," she said. "Eleven feet tall. You?"

The Douglas Fir section was a long ways back. He hoped he'd have the wherewithal to drag the tree back to the road for her. "I'm opting for a blue spruce," he said, choosing the kind of tree closest to the road. "But we'll get yours first."

"Deal."

She smiled, and he just basked in her for a second. The sun was beaming down on her hair, the chilly breeze lifting it and playing with its curls, and her eyes were like a chocolate bar in the sun. Her cheeks were pink from the cold, and it made her even more beautiful to him.

"What?" she asked after a moment.

He shook his head. "You're just pretty enough to take a man's breath away, is all."

Her smile seemed to falter. She lowered her eyes.

"What's wrong, Vidalia?"

"Nothing. I...." She sighed. "Nothing. I mean, there *is* something. But I don't want to ruin our day with it. So I'm gonna put it out of my mind and just enjoy this. And being with you."

"Is there someone else?" he asked, because he couldn't stand not to know.

She looked him right in the eyes. "There's never been anyone else, Bobby Joe. You said you never got me outta your mind.

Well, I need to be honest and admit that I never got you outta mine either. I never will."

A little rush of alarm went through him. He lowered his head, guilt rising up in his chest. He should tell her. He didn't expect her to return his feelings at all, much less this quickly, this easily. Her words to him were a dream come true, but it just wasn't fair. He had to tell her. He couldn't let her fall in love with him before she knew he was dying.

He couldn't.

"I never got over you, Bobby Joe. And I don't imagine I ever will. But I did a bad thing to you way back then, and I've got to make it right with you now. Before we go any further. I've got to tell you–"

"There's something I've got to tell you too, Vidalia," he said very softly. He met her eyes, dreading that discussion. And then a father walked past them, dragging a pine tree and carrying a little girl on his shoulders, and they were laughing their way through a chorus of Jingle Bells. Bobby smiled and felt lighter. "But not today," he said. "Today, let's just get some Christmas trees, have fun, and not worry about anything heavy. Okay?"

She smiled brightly. "That is more than okay," she told him.

The scene in the parking lot in front of the Long Branch Saloon was like something out of an old western film. The five daughters of Vidalia Brand stood shoulder to shoulder facing the three sons of Bobby Joe McIntyre. About ten feet of recently laid blacktop stretched between them.

Kara Brand had made the call asking for this meeting. Jason had felt bristly, like his family was about to be accused of something and had expected a hostile encounter. He hadn't been all that worried about it, though. At least not until he'd seen them.

He and his brothers might as well have been face to face

with a gang of super models. The apples had not fallen far from the tree in this family. Robert and Joey were as rocked by their beauty as he was, but he hoped they also noticed that every last one of them was wearing a wedding ring. Off limits. The McIntyre's didn't roll that way. If there was one thing their father had managed to drum into them during their upbringing, it was that you didn't so much as flirt with a married woman. Hell, not even a going steady girl, when they'd been in high school. It was probably the one item in their father's moral code that stood above all others.

A handful of cars came and went, and he didn't miss their sudden deceleration or the rubber necking drivers.

Finally, he cleared his throat and walked closer, extending a hand to the apparent leader, "I'm Jason McIntyre."

"Maya Brand." She smiled a little stiffly and shook his hand with a respectably firm grip.

"These are my brothers, Robert and Joseph," he said, indicating the two men who flanked him.

"My sisters," she replied. "Edie, Kara, Melusine and Selene." She nodded at each girl as she named them.

His defensiveness relaxed a little. "Those are all names of goddesses, aren't they?"

"Mama had high expectations for her daughters," Maya said. "Robert, are you named for your father?"

Rob said, "We all are. Dad's full name is Jason Robert Joseph."

More traffic passed, slowed. More drivers gaped.

"We don't get inside soon, there's gonna be a crowd gathered," Melusine said. "And if we're gonna have a shootout, it oughtta be at the OK Corral, so we might as well talk instead."

Nodding, getting her attempt at levity, but not thinking it very funny, Jason led the way, held the door for the females and let them enter first. The youngest one, the platinum blonde with the very blue eyes, looked around in wide-eyed appreciation. "This place is amazing. Wow, is that a player piano?"

"It is," Joey said, sounding proud. Of the three of them, he was the one who was eating all this up. He loved finally being included in one of their father's projects and was diving head-long into the whole outlaw skit nonsense Dad had planned for them. It wasn't surprising. Joey was the fun-loving kid of the family, and he was taking Selene to show her the piano, tinkling the keys and pointing out the hidden controls.

Robert was harder to read. He'd always been laid back, easy going, never had strong opinions about much of anything. But his go-with-the-flow attitude had been replaced by heartbreak recently when his long-time girlfriend had jilted him.

Jason didn't imagine their father's news was going to be easy for either of his brothers to take.

"Pick a table, ladies," Joey called, going behind the bar for the tray of cookies he had waiting. "I raided the kitchen after you called. Bring that coffee, will you Rob?"

Robert nodded and picked up a carafe from the pot behind the bar. The youngest Brand girl, Selene, slid onto a barstool and said, "We don't need a table, the bar's just fine." Then she ran a hand over it and nodded. "Real fine."

One of the sisters elbowed her, Melusine, if he had them straight. "We're here to talk about our mother and your father."

"And if our mother knew it, she'd probably disown us," one of the two tall ones put in. Edie or Kara. Edie he thought, but either one could be the former model. Heck, any of them could. "So we'd appreciate your discretion."

Joey frowned and looked at Jason. In fact, Robert was looking at him too. Jason sighed. "My brothers only arrived this morning. I haven't filled them in yet, and to tell you the truth, I probably know less than any of you ladies."

"Wait, wait, wait, now. Our father and their mother–" Joey began.

"Didn't you get the last name, Joe? Brand. Their mother is *Vidalia* Brand," Jason said.

70

"*Holeee* smokes." That was Robert. He was looking at one of the glossy flyers with her likeness on it. An open box of them still sat on the bar, the few left that Jason and his dad hadn't plastered all over town already.

The women were frowning from one to the other. Kara said, "You know our mother?"

"Know *of* her," Joey said. "Dad's...mentioned her."

"Might as well be honest, Joe. Dad's kind of obsessed with her."

"Robert–" Jason's voice had a warning tone.

"C'mon, Jay, these girls are clearly concerned about whatever is going on here. They have a right to know the truth, don't they?"

"*You* don't even know the truth," his older brother muttered.

Maya was still standing. She moved behind the bar to help Joey put out cups and saucers, found the creamer in the mini-fridge down low, while he grabbed a box of sugar packets and set it out.

"None of us know the whole truth," she said. "Our mother's been keeping secrets, and that's not like her." Then she sighed. "This can't be easy for you to discuss. I'm sure your loyalty lies with your mother–"

"Our parents' divorce was the best thing for both of them. They were both happier afterward, which meant we were as well. And Mom's happily married to a guy who's crazy about her now," Robert said.

Jason took the carafe and filled a mug, passed it to Maya, then filled another and offered it to Selene.

"There's always been another woman on Dad's mind," Joey mused softly. "The one that got away. The one he never got over. The most stunning beauty west of the Mississippi. Sweet Vidalia Brand." He gave the words dramatic flair with a hand on his chest and a faraway look in his eyes.

"What's your mother's...situation?" Robert asked.

"What do you mean, *situation?*" Melusine returned. Jason knew which one she was, because he'd seen her photograph online when he'd been checking into this family. She and her husband Alex were high priced P.I.s.

Robert lifted his brows. "Relationship-wise."

Maya said, "My father-in-law's half in love with her."

"So's my brother in law," said the youngest, which made Jason lift his eyebrows in surprise.

"And don't forget Reverend Jackson," Kara put in.

Mel shrugged. "But Mama hasn't shown much interest in any of them."

"Still, nothing could possibly have ever happened between them in the past," Kara said. "Mom was still married to Daddy when she knew Bobby Joe. Right?" She blinked from one of her sisters to another.

Selene shrugged. "Don't ask me. It was before I was born."

"She was married," Maya stated it flatly.

Mel shook her head. "She thought she was married. But it was never legal. Our father already had a wife when he married our mother. We're all bastards, if you want to know the truth of it."

Jason heard more underneath the words, but decided not to pry. His father's warnings about never looking twice at a married woman, however, were suddenly taking on a whole new meaning. Maybe he'd been speaking from experience.

"Wow, that's one for the history books, isn't it?" Joey asked. He was leaning on the bar, listening raptly. "So where's your father now?" Joey asked.

Robert's jaw ticked a little bit.

"Shot by gangsters," Selene said in a dramatic tone. "Aren't we just the most scandalous bunch you've ever met?"

She was a lot like Joey, Jason thought. No carburetor.

"It's not funny, Selene." Her oldest sister sent her a look. "His other wife was killed as well, and for a time, we thought their

72

two kids with them, though it turns out they got away. We only just reunited with them a few years ago."

"He deserved what those gangsters did to him," Selene said. "He was a piece of–"

"Selene!" Maya snapped.

Selene rolled her eyes at her eldest sister, but she closed her mouth.

"My mother's a good woman, a church-going woman," Maya said then. "She wouldn't have broken her marriage vows, even though they were to a man who didn't deserve her."

"And speaking of church, she should've been back by now, and she'll expect to see us at the house." Melusine looked uneasily toward the door.

Kara shook her head. "No, she won't be back yet. She was going to pick out a Christmas tree for the Corral after church."

Jason and his brothers exchanged a quick look, and the girls sent them a questioning one. Might as well tell them, Jason thought. "That's what dad said he was doing when he left here. Going to get a Christmas tree for the saloon."

"Holy smokes," Joey said again. "There really *is* something going on here, isn't there?" He picked up one of the flyers, nodding as he perused it. "Who can blame him though? If she's as pretty in person–"

"I don't think that's it." Jason snatched the flyer away and dropped it back into the box. "Dad's got...a lot going on."

"Yeah," Mel said, getting to her feet. "Like selling off assets and closing businesses."

"You sound like you suspect him of something," Jason said, sliding off his barstool as well and facing her. His father hadn't been the best, but he would be damned if he'd let some strange female accuse him of anything. The man was dying, for God's sake.

Kara got up and planted herself right in between them, a

palm to each chest. "Mel, lots of people decide to close businesses. It's called retirement. It doesn't mean anything dire."

Jason said, "I'm curious how you know so much about my father's business. You and your P.I. husband investigate him or something?"

"Yeah, just like you apparently investigated us, or you wouldn't know we were P.I.s at all," she shot back.

"Whoa, now," Joey said. He clapped a firm hand on Jason's shoulder, as if he was going to physically set him on his ass if he didn't back down. "Look, ladies, we're as in the dark here as you are," Joey said. "It's just not like our father, this behavior. His business is everything to him. It's been his whole life. We had no idea he was liquidating everything. And then he heads out here and buys this place in the middle of nowhere. And not to flip it for profit, either, Jason says. It's just...he's never done that. If I didn't know better, I'd think he intends to stay here, long term." He looked at his brothers. "Maybe he's serious about Vidalia Brand."

The door opened, and a happy couple came in backwards, laughing and dragging what had to be an eighteen-foot tree behind them. The woman fell on her backside and smiled up at the man. And he beamed down at her as if she was the mother of all goddesses. And maybe she was at that, Jason thought.

And then their laughter died as they both realized they weren't alone, and turned their gazes toward the summit meeting at the bar.

"Well now, what have we here?" Vidalia asked as Bobby Joe closed his hand around hers and helped her to her feet.

Jason's father met his eyes, asking him without a word how much he had told these women, not to mention his brothers. Bobby Joe took three steps closer, and then he collapsed in a heap on the floor.

CHAPTER SIX

"*B*obby!" Vidalia dropped to her knees beside him as the sum total of their offspring stampeded closer. Maya was the first to dial 911. Vidalia heard her on the phone with the dispatcher, but she didn't think Bobby was very likely to let any ambulance take him out of here. She laid her head on his chest and felt his heart beating nice and strong and steady. His breathing seemed okay, too.

And then his hand touched her hair, and she opened her wet eyes, lifted her head and met his.

He gave her a wavering smile. "I'm not going to any hospital, Vidalia. I'm fine. Trust me."

"You were unconscious." She looked up at his sons. The two younger ones looked stunned and terrified, but the eldest had gone white and she thought a stiff breeze might knock him over. "Has anything like this happened before?"

"Never," Joey said. But Jason didn't say a word.

"I'm fine. It's okay, I'm fine now." Bobby Joe pushed himself up until he was sitting instead of lying flat. Vidalia held his shoulders, searched his eyes, read them, and knew in that moment that what had just happened was not a surprise to him. He already knew what was wrong. And he knew what he was doing.

"Maya, call Doc Shelby," she said. "He'll be home. He's retired. Get him over here pronto. He'll be faster than an ambulance anyway. You boys, help your father upstairs and get him into a bed."

No one even thought to argue with her. People seldom did. Vidalia had been through enough emergencies to be able to handle herself in the midst of one. But she couldn't get her head to stop spinning with a million questions. If he was sick and he hadn't told her, then it had to be one of two things. Either it was nothing at all or it was damned serious.

The boys helped their father to his feet, because he wouldn't let them carry him. He slung an arm around Jason, and nodded back at the other two. "Rob, Joey, get the tree upright and into a stand, will you? There's a big one over there by the windows in front. It'll look spectacular from outside, once we get the lights strung."

The boys clearly knew something was going on.

So did Vidalia. She and Jason flanked Bobby Joe, but he looked at her next, smiled and it was a real smile. "I have no intention of missing that Sunday Dinner you promised me."

"We'll just see what Doc Shelby says."

"All right," he told her. "You bring him on upstairs when he gets here, will you Vidalia?"

She blinked. He was asking her to stay down here. He wanted time alone with his firstborn. Hell, what was going on with him?

She didn't ask though. Not now. She smiled, knowing it didn't reach her eyes, and nodded, and kept her tear spigot turned off. "All right."

Jason helped his father up the stairs. When they were out of sight, Vidalia turned and saw seven younger sets of eyes staring at her, as if maybe she had the answers. She shook her head slowly. "I'm sorry, gang. I don't know what's wrong with him either, and I'm as worried as you are."

"Maybe he just pushed himself too hard," Selene said, staring up the stairway even though there was no longer anyone on it. "That tree must have been heavy."

"That's why he picked his from the bunch nearest the road, I'll bet," Vidalia muttered, kicking herself. "God, mine was almost halfway back, and he dragged it all the way for me."

"Shouldn't have been a problem," Robert said. "Dad's a young man."

"He's in better shape than I am," Joey said, patting his flat belly as if it wasn't.

"He's never had a spell like this before?" Vidalia asked the men.

"Never," Joey said.

"Never that we know of," Robert added, sending a suspicious look up the stairs.

Vidalia got the feeling that young man was starting to have the same worries that she was. When a man sold all he had, closed his business, and went back to the town and the woman he'd long since left behind, maybe he had reasons. He'd said there was something he hadn't told her.

Well, there was something she hadn't told him, too, and once Doc finished up with him, she knew she had to. There was no more time for waiting around. Reverend Jackson was right. She'd have tanned her daughters' hides if they'd kept the secrets she had.

She looked at her girls, shook her head. "I've got a tree out there needs taking to the Corral. And I hope to the good Lord someone remembered to turn off my pot roast."

~

"Never been so embarrassed in my life," he muttered as the local medic gave him the once over. "Dropped just like a sack of feed, right in front of the prettiest woman in creation."

The retired medico who insisted Bobby Joe call him Doc, just smiled at him, his teeth too white and even to belong in such a well-lined face. His hair was shock white and curly. He smelled like peppermint and looked like Mark Twain.

"You don't seem at all concerned," Doc said when he'd finished listening to Bobby Joe's chest, poking and prodding his belly, taking his blood pressure, and shining a bright light into his eyes.

"I'm not, Doc. You're just here for show. I know exactly what's wrong with me, and I'm not ready for anyone else to know. When I am, they will."

Doc lifted his eyebrows. "There might be something I can do—"

"There's not." He sat up in the bed, feeling like himself again.

"You do realize that anything you tell me stays between us, don't you? I may be retired, but my oath isn't."

Bobby Joe liked the old fellow. "I do know that. I also know that if you walk out of this room looking morose, no one's gonna quit prodding me until I give them some answers. And I'm saving that for after the holidays."

"So it's bad, then. Bone marrow transplant won't do the trick?"

He felt his eyes widen on the older man.

Doc shrugged. "You'd be surprised what a good doctor can tell from an external exam."

Sighing, Bobby gave in. "I'm on the list. None of my sons are compatible."

Doc nodded. "How far advanced are you?"

"They gave me three months and that was three months ago. I just want to have a nice, hometown kind of Christmas with my family before I have to break the news. That's all. Just one old-fashioned family holiday. The kind I never gave them. So please, leave this room with a smile on your face and make it convincing."

Doc nodded slow. "You've got it." He heaved a big sigh, extended a hand. "It's a pleasure to meet you, Mr. McIntyre. I only wish—"

"Nice to meet you, too." Bobby Joe swung his legs around and put his sock feet on the floor, so he'd be sitting up, not lying down in the bed when the door opened. "Merry Christmas, Doc."

"Merry Christmas." He opened the door, lifted his head and put on a smile for the crowd gathered in the hall outside it. Three strapping men, and Vidalia standing among them, a foot shorter and a mile prettier. Of them all, only Jason knew the truth, and he was standing there waiting, probably expecting Doc Shelby to share the grim news with them all and ruin the holiday for everyone.

Instead, Doc said, "Can't find a thing wrong with him, but I did extract a promise he'd come see me once the holidays are over."

Jason frowned and looked past the doctor to his dad, who told him without a word to keep quiet. Just a look, and Jason read it, pressed his lips, but then gave a nod so slight no one but Bobby Joe could've seen it.

Vidalia didn't look convinced, and she came inside, marched right up to the bed, clasped his face between her palms and stared hard into his eyes. Her dark brown ones were filled with questions, speculation, and worry.

"I'm holding you to that Sunday dinner invitation, Vidalia Brand," Bobby Joe said.

"Well that's good, because I'm bringing it here. This place needs a good breaking in before you throw it open to an unsuspecting public."

"You don't have to—"

"Don't start with me, Jason Robert Joseph McIntyre. And after dinner, we're gonna decorate that tree of yours. I presume you have some ornaments around here somewhere."

He smiled at her, at the way she was taking charge and making this about anything and everything other than his health. "I do. I've been doing a lot of shopping in between flirting with you every chance I get."

She rolled her eyes, pretended a lightness he knew she wasn't feeling. She'd question him later, when they were alone, he thought. But for now, she was putting on a show for his sake and for his sons. "I've got to go get everything together. You boys," she said, addressing his sons, "You might want to child-proof the place just a little. Put anything breakable out of reach, and set your mechanical bull to Slow."

She leaned down and pressed a kiss to Bobby's mouth, not caring what his sons might think about that. "I'll see you in a couple of hours. I want you to rest until then."

Then she turned and left, her steps brisk and purposeful all the way down the hall, down the stairs, and out the front door. He heard her pickup start and heard her drive away. Shaking his head, he looked at his sons. "That right there is one hell of a woman, boys. And you might as well know now as later, I love her. I've loved her most of my life."

Vidalia Brand was nobody's fool. She'd raised five girls practically on her own, so she knew bullshit when she saw it. Doc had been shoveling it when he'd come out of Bobby Joe's room, and Bobby Joe had been dealing it all along.

He was not well. She'd managed to put it all together while directing his sons to raise that Christmas tree, get it upright, straight, and properly placed.

When she arrived at home, the family was already there, every last one of them. The twins were running in and out of the living room, hanging a fresh batch of ornaments, freshly made for her in their pre-school class, on her tree. Tyler was keeping right up with them, helping them reach the higher branches. The braces he'd once worn on his legs were a thing of the past, and while he still walked with a slight limp, he was on his way to complete healing.

The men, her sons in law, were gathered in the living room, sipping beers, talking and watching the kids, while the girls were in the kitchen, bustling. Every Sunday was like a holiday around here.

When she walked in, everyone went silent and looked her way.

"How is he, Mama?" Selene asked.

Vidalia took a deep breath and decided to respect Bobby Joe's wishes by not sharing her suspicions just yet. "Doc Shelby said he couldn't find a thing wrong with him. Just a fluke, I think." Selene's eyes said she knew better, but Vidalia hurried on. "If you will all indulge me, I would like to take our Sunday Dinner over to the Long Branch."

"If that's what you want, Mom, sure we will," Melusine said.

"It won't even be hard," Maya added. "We've got the sides all made already."

"We can wrap everything up to keep it warm," Edie put in

Vidalia frowned at them. "Why are you being so cooperative all of the sudden?"

Kara came and put a hand on her mother's shoulder. "We saw your face when he went down in a heap, Mama. We know you...have feelings for him."

"Well, don't be ridiculous, I don't have any...well...I suppose I am *fond* of the man, but it's not as if... it's not as if...." She shook her head. "Let's just get this food over there, all right?"

The girls exchanged knowing looks and everyone started loading pans, kids and themselves into the vehicles that cluttered Vidalia's driveway. Selene alone hung back, waving her beloved Cory away when he came for her. That was something, because the two were inseparable. But Cory seemed to understand, and he stepped outside, leaving the two alone together in the house. Selene closed the front door, and turning, stared into Vidalia's eyes.

"He's sick, isn't he, Mama?"

Vidalia was, by now, used to her youngest daughter's odd ways. She knew things, Selene did. There was no point in lying to her. "I think so. But I also think he doesn't want anyone to know."

"I could sense it. Something out of balance in him. Is there anything we can do?"

Vidalia nodded. "We can pray for him, child. I in my way, and you in yours."

"As hard as I can," she told her mom, and then she hugged her softly, and Vidalia had all she could do not to let her worried tears break free.

Bobby Joe's sons had set up the banquet room for dinner. It had gold wallpaper with velvet textured swirls and roses. It was set off from the rest of the saloon by red velvet curtains with gold tassels that could be drawn for privacy. It would be crowded, as Vidalia's family was huge. Vidalia, her five daughters, three grandkids, five sons in law, added to Bobby's three sons, and himself made eighteen—quite a crowd for a meal.

The long table was set though, with him at the head, Vidalia at the foot, eight chairs on each side. And when the food was all laid out, wafting scents that made his mouth water, and everyone had taken their seats, an odd, tense silence made the very air in the room feel heavy.

And then Vidalia said, "So, Tyler, why don't you tell us all what you've asked Santa Claus to bring you for Christmas?"

The little boy grinned. "A pony! And I think he's gonna do it this year, I really do. I've been so good, and I know how to take care of him. Miss Haggerty teaches me every single week when I go out to ride Rusty. And I can board him at her place and ride him anytime I want."

"If you get one, can the twins come and ride too?" Maya asked. Her kids started bouncing in their seats, asking "Can we, can we?" They were smack between her and Caleb, so they could keep them anchored and focused.

"Sure you can!" Tyler said, nodding eagerly. "I'll show you everything. I know how to put on a saddle, and a bridle, and—"

"I want a baby. A real one, not make believe," Dahlia said.

Maya and Caleb looked at each other in surprise, but their little girl went right on. "I got so many dolls. I'm tired of dolls. I want a *real* baby."

"I want a four wheeler," her brother said. He was all of four years old.

"Over my dead body." Vidalia pressed a hand to her chest. "You'll get yourself killed."

"Oh, I don't know, Vidalia," Bobby Joe put in. "I think Joey had one at his age."

"I sure did," Joey boasted, grinning at CC. "It was red, and Dad put a control on it so it wouldn't go faster than he thought I could handle. But my big brother Robby knew how to take it off."

"Oh, you didn't!" Vidalia shot a wide-eyed look at Robert.

He smiled, apparently remembering. "I did."

"Yep, he sure did," Jason said with a frown at his brothers. "And within the hour, Joey drove it into a tree and wound up with eighteen stitches in his head."

Maya shot Caleb a terrified look. Caleb patted her hand. "They have little ones that barely go five miles an hour, hon. Far more suited to a four-year-old."

Soon they were all exchanging childhood memories, and eventually, Christmas memories. Maya told about the birth of the twins the year of that freak snowstorm. Kara talked about her first Christmas with Tyler and Jimmy, leaving out the scary parts involving Jim's addict ex and her porn-king boyfriend. At that point, Bobby Joe's boys seemed to run out of tales of their own to offer, and Vidalia shot a look across the table at him, about to try to prompt him for some more, he thought.

"I want a Christmas like that, this year," he said. "Well, minus the blizzard and home delivery of twins, that is." Everyone laughed softly and beamed at Maya and Caleb. Then Bobby went on. "I want an old-fashioned holiday, full of pine needles and piles of food and noisy family members all talking at once."

"Kind of like this right here, right now, you mean?" Vidalia asked him.

Smiling, he nodded hard. "Just like this." He looked at his sons. "That's part of the reason I asked you boys to come up here. So we could have that together, right here in Big Falls. My adopted hometown. That's how I've thought of it ever since I left it behind."

"I think that's a beautiful idea," Vidalia said. "And I'd be real pleased if we could have that together, Bobby. You and your boys are welcome to share your holidays with us."

"I was hoping you'd say that." He lifted a glass. "To family."

"To family," Vidalia agreed, and they all lifted their glasses in agreement. Even the children picked up their glasses of juice and tinked them together.

Bobby met Vidalia's eyes across the table and held them as their families all started talking at once and food was passed around and compliments were paid. And he couldn't help thinking that this should've been *their* family. His and hers. They should've been spending *every* holiday season all gathered around together, all talking at once with kids making a mess of their food and dreaming of ponies and babies and Santa Claus.

When the meal ended, he left their offspring to clean up the mess, and took Vidalia with him into the main part of the saloon. The eighteen-foot tree stood bare and waiting. "We're gonna deck these halls tonight. Then, dessert by the fireplace. Will you stay?"

"You couldn't get me out of here if you tried, Bobby Joe."

He smiled at her, and he knew he was going to have to tell her the truth pretty soon. But maybe it could wait just a few more nights. Just a few. He wanted a Christmas without heartache. One so chock full of joy and sappy holiday magic that his sons would never forget it. He wanted that, just once, before he died.

They all stood around the eighteen-foot beauty of a tree, and Bobby Joe said, "I bought decorations, but I don't think there's gonna be anywhere near enough."

"Don't worry about that," Selene said, walking right up beside him and resting her hand on his shoulder. "Mom had us bring a small portion of the horde of holiday decor she had stashed at home in the attic."

"I think we have enough for ten trees," Vidalia said. "Plus two." She gazed at the boxes, smiling in self-deprecation. "Some of these haven't seen daylight in several years. I can't wait to go through them. Shall we?"

"Lights first," Caleb called. "We have to string the lights first. That's how we always do it."

"I'm with you on that Caleb," Jason said.

"Fine, you young men handle the lights," Vidalia told him. "Robert, can you find us a couple of stepladders around here?"

"Yes, ma'am," Robert said. And if Bobby Joe didn't know better, he would think Rob was starting to enjoy himself a bit. His sadness seemed distant, and he was even smiling now and then.

Melusine cranked up the music. Caleb and Rob strung the lights, while Vidalia gave constant direction. The others girls vanished into the kitchen. But in short order, they were back, handing cups of hot cocoa around. Jimmy, Kara's husband, turned up the music a little louder, and when Randy Travis started singing Rudolf the Red-Nosed Reindeer, the children all sang along.

They were are all picking through boxes of ornaments, re-attaching hooks or strings, and passing them around to be placed on the tree. And it seemed to Bobby Joe that every single piece in Vidalia's old dusty boxes from the attic had a story attached to it. Her girls didn't mind one bit telling them as each one was added to the tree.

He heard all about the Christmas when they'd all made homemade gifts for each other because money was low, but how somehow, they'd still found Cabbage Patch dolls under the tree, one for each of those girls, from Santa.

"You never told us how you did it, Mama," Maya said softly.

"I got up at two a.m. on Black Friday to be first in line at the Kmart, where they had a five doll limit. I pawned my wedding ring to pay for them." She rolled her eyes. "Oh your father was furious when he came home and saw my ring finger bare. Course, by then it was February, and I'd saved up enough to buy it back."

Selene pulled out an ornament, a picture frame shaped like Santa's sleigh with a baby in the seat beside Santa. "This was me!" she said happily. "Look!" She held it up.

"Baby's first Christmas" was part of the frame itself. But

someone had taken a green marker and carefully inscribed "Selene Brand," and her birthday.

She grinned and handed it to Joey. "We always joke that I was conceived by the Corral. Born nine months to the day after her doors opened."

"Yeah, Barroom Baby," said Melusine.

"Saloon Sister!" Kara threw in.

"Beer Barrel Brat," Maya called.

"Happy Hour Half-Pint," Edie sang.

"Enough already!" Selene said, but she was laughing so hard she had tears brimming in her eyes, and she was leaning on her husband Cory as if she'd fall down without him. He was laughing too.

Bobby Joe frowned though, and sent a searching look Vidalia's way, but she averted her eyes.

"She was a premie."

"An eight-pound premie," Edie said. "Good thing she came early, or Ma still wouldn't be walking straight."

Mel snorted, elbowing Alex, her quiet, well-dressed husband whose sharp eyes seemed to see everything, and everyone laughed. Then the next ornament came out of the box, and another story came with it. No one seemed overly stuck on Selene's tale. No one but Bobby Joe. He was kind of fixated on it and spent the rest of the evening searching the girl and noticing things that probably meant nothing at all.

Her eyes, though, weren't they a lot like Joey's? The shape of them, at least. And her chin was almost identical to Jason's. But no, she looked like her sisters too, and like her mother. All in different ways.

Still....

No. No, Vidalia wouldn't have kept a secret like that. Not like that.

Would she?

He watched when the ornament with her baby photo was

hung, and sidled that way at the first opportunity for a closer look. But Vidalia reached past him, and took it from the branch where it dangled. "Sorry, Bobby Joe, but this one ought to be on my tree at home. I have no idea why it was buried in that box of forgotten ornaments."

"You're the one who keeps saying everything happens for a reason, Vidalia," he said. "Could there have been a reason for that, too?"

She averted her eyes. "My forgetfulness is the only one that comes to mind. Oh, look! Kara, that's the God's Eye you made in Kindergarten!" And she hurried to her daughter and left the conversation with Bobby Joe unfinished.

But a seed had been planted, and he was looking at Selene differently now, and at the easy way she was laughing with Joey and rearranging the glittering silver ball he'd just hung.

When the tree was all decked, Vidalia ran around shutting off all the lights, and Rob stood with a plug in one hand, near an outlet. Everyone else gathered in front of the giant pine. The children were still giggly but starting to look a little bit sleepy, too.

As soon as Vidalia returned to his side, Bobby Joe said, "Okay, Rob. Light her up."

Rob plugged in the extension cord, and the tree came to life, a collection of multicolored lights, topped by strand after strand of tiny white twinkling ones. There came a collective "Ooooh" that should've been corny, but somehow, wasn't.

Softly, Maya started to sing "Oh Christmas Tree" and the others all joined in. Even his sons, though they probably had to guess at the words. Vidalia elbowed him. "Come on, open that heart of yours and let the magic in."

He nodded and started singing. He didn't mutter. He sang out loud. And he knew he was going to get his wish. A Christmas his sons could remember after he was gone. And all thanks to this woman.

Even as he thought it, she looked up at him with a dreamy smile and a suspicious glimmer on her lashes, and slipped her small hand inside his. He closed his around it, and his heart tightened. It wasn't fair not to tell her. He realized he had to do it and soon. He was going to break her heart otherwise.

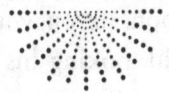

CHAPTER SEVEN

*V*idalia said she had posted signs all over the OK Corral explaining that tonight, she was closing in order to help welcome a new saloon to town and encouraging her patrons to stop in to see her at the grand opening of The Long Branch.

Now she was with him, at the brand new saloon, and she and the boys were rehearsing their lines in the store rooms in back. Bobby Joe had spared no expense on the costumes and props. Vidalia had even added Miss Kitty's beauty mark to her own cheek for good measure. She looked more like Miss Kitty than the real one had, aside from one minor alteration. Vidalia's hair was jet black, not copper penny red.

Her big skirt and bustier top might have been a little sexier than Miss Kitty had worn, but then, he'd probably think that about a feedbag if she was the one wearing it. "Marshall Dillon" walked up behind her and looked over her shoulder at her reflection. He couldn't keep his eyes off her décolletage and didn't bother trying. "Damn, woman. You look even better in that getup than that photo of you from Halloween."

"Well, it's a nicer costume," she said, but her eyes were on him in the mirror. He wore his duster and cowboy hat and her eyes said she liked the look on him.

"Even better than you did in my imagination when I picked it out, too, he went on, as if she hadn't spoken. "And trust me, that's saying something."

"I'm not bad for my age, I suppose."

"You're not bad for any age." He turned toward the still-open door leading into the saloon. "Jason, you out there?"

"Yeah, pop," Jason said, poking his head through the door. "What's up?"

Bobby Joe pulled his six shooter from his holster and held it up. "You're gonna have to switch out my blanks for real bullets, or I'm not gonna be able to keep the competition away from my lady, here."

Vidalia spun around, snatched the gun away from him. "Keep it in your holster, Marshall."

He laughed out loud, slapping his thigh, and Jason laughed too, shaking his head and returning to the saloon.

"You look so much better than you did the other day," Vidalia said, her smile giving way to a serious expression, and a searching one too.

"I feel better. You make me feel better."

She looked as if she was about to say more, even opened her mouth, but then closed it again, and he could almost hear her thoughts. *Not tonight. Tonight's the grand opening. It can wait.*

To ensure she didn't change her mind, he went to the door, pushed it open a little and peeked out. "Man, the place is jumping, and it's still early." They would repeat their floor show twice tonight, and it was nearly time for the first run.

"I'm glad. I want the Long Branch to be successful, Bobby."

"Not afraid I'm gonna put you outta business anymore?" he asked.

She shook her head firmly. "No. You were right, it's an entirely different sort of place. I think it'll complement mine, not compete with it. Yours is for tourists and special occasions. Mine's for the locals. I'm sorry I didn't believe you in the beginning."

He shrugged, letting the door fall closed and facing her fully. "You've got nothing to be sorry for, Vidalia."

"Oh yes I do, Bobby Joe. And I'm gonna tell you all about it...soon. But not tonight." She heard the gasp of the crowd and then the sounds of Joey's grand entrance as he burst into the saloon through the batwing doors, shooting his guns in the air and growling, "Hand over the cash, barkeep!" The barkeep was Robert, who hadn't wanted to play, but had agreed to tend bar and at least put his hands up and act scared when the villain burst in.

"You're on, Miss Kitty," Bobby Joe said. "Head on out there."

"I'm nervous, can you believe it?" She headed for the door, and Bobby Joe attempted to smack her on the backside as she passed, but the layers of slips and crinoline prevented it from amounting to much.

Then she made her entrance, sashaying across the saloon to the center of the floor, where an area had been cleared of tables for this to play out. She put her hands on her hips and a heap of attitude into her tone as she called, "Just what do you think you're doin', Mister? Put those guns down before I show you a new place to keep 'em."

Feigning shock, then pushing his hat back a bit and admiring her much like his father had just done, Joey said, "Well now, ma'am, far be it from me to insult a beautiful lady, but I got business here."

"If your business is robbing this saloon, then it's my business too. Now put those guns away and get out of here before I do what your mama should'a done years ago."

"And what would that be, ma'am?"

"Oh, I'll show you what that would be." She had, by that time, maneuvered her way to the authentically aged braided leather bull whip that was curled up and hanging on the wall, and she yanked it down and gave it a snap that cracked deliciously.

Technically, Miss Kitty had never used a bull whip in *Gunsmoke*. It was Barbara Stanwick as Victoria Barclay who had often put bad guys in their places with a whip back in the days of *The Big Valley*, but Bobby Joe had taken a bit of poetic license, and Vidalia agreed it was a nice effect.

As she swung the whip for a second time, Joey caught it and jerked her forward, pulling her around in front of him and turning them both to face the doors just as Bobby Joe, dressed as Matt Dillon walked in, drew his gun, and ordered, "Let the lady go, pard." He'd gone out the back door and come around the front to make his entrance, just as planned.

"Drop your gun or I'll drop your woman, Marshall."

"Don't listen, Matthew!" Vidalia cried. "Shoot him in the head. You won't miss!"

"Yeah, *Matthew*. Shoot me in the head, and maybe hit her instead. Or put your gun down," Joey drawled.

Bobby Joe lowered his gun. Vidalia stomped on (beside, actually) Joey's foot, then spun away from him, and Bobby brought his gun level again and fired twice.

Joey jerked with each blast, got one shot off that went astray, knocking a painting off the wall—it was rigged. Behind the scenes, Jason had simply pulled a cord that sent the picture to the floor. It took Joey five minutes to finally die, and even after he hit the floor he kept kicking and gasping for a while. But he finally ended it. Saloon girl Selene was ruining the ruse by giggling at his antics behind her gloved hand.

Matt Dillon swept Miss Kitty into his arms, bent over her and kissed the living daylights out of her while the crowd whooped and roared. The piano player started tickling the ivories again, and a couple of dusty cowboys (Cory and Jimmy) came in and dragged Joey out of the bar.

But Vidalia wasn't paying attention anymore. She was in

Bobby's arms and that was right where he wanted her to be. When he lifted his head, she stared into his eyes. "That wasn't in the script," she whispered.

"It is now."

"Bobby, I have something I've got to tell you. And it can't wait any longer."

He frowned and set her upright again. Then taking off his hat and waving it at the still cheering patrons, he scooped her up into his arms and strode right out the front door, and around to the rear of the saloon.

There wasn't much out there, Vidalia thought. A patch of scrub brush, bare ground, and a creek meandering along a few yards back. That was where he carried her, despite her protests. And when he set her down on her feet again, he kept his hands around her waist. "You look so good as Miss Kitty I can't take my eyes off you. No one could."

"Oh, stop it Bobby Joe. This is serious." She lowered her head, unable to look him in the eye. "I should have told you a long time ago. But I just.... I was so ashamed."

He frowned, his playful expression giving way to a worried one. Then he led her a little farther, where a wooden bench had been placed along the bank of the creek.

"Here. Sit. If you can, in that skirt."

She bunched its layers up, checked the bench for dirt, and not seeing any, took his advice and sat down. He sat beside her. "I like to come out here and just watch the water go by," he said. "It's soothing."

"Water's like that for me, too. It's a nice spot. The whole thing, what you've done here, with this place. It's really amazing, Bobby. It's wonderful. You did all right."

"You think the boys liked it?" he asked, his eyes searching hers.

"Joey sure did. He almost convinced me he was a real outlaw."

"Yeah, yeah." He nodded, eyes low. "But do they like the place? I built it for them, you know. I want to leave them something more than just a portfolio full of stocks and holdings. I want to leave them something real. Something they can build on, be proud of. You know, when I go."

"Which isn't gonna be for another thirty years or so." She frowned at him. "Is it?"

He smiled as if she'd said something funny. "You said you had something to tell me. You trying to change the subject now?"

She wasn't. But she thought maybe he was, and she filed it away to mull on later, with all the other little things leading her to a conclusion she didn't want to reach. But first, she had to come clean. Entirely clean. Because she was falling in love with this man. Again. Maybe she'd never really fallen out of it.

Drawing a deep breath, she nodded once, lifted her chin and met his eyes. "I lied to you all those years ago, Bobby. That night we spent together? The night you can't remember?"

He nodded, but didn't speak.

"I told you I didn't remember either. But I did. And I still do. I remember every single second of it. And it was...it was the most beautiful, the most intimate night of my entire life. You made me feel...cherished. And I didn't want it to end."

He sat up straighter and searched her eyes. "Are you saying that we–?"

"We made love. We made sweet, incredible love." She pressed her lips tight, nodded once. "And there's more...."

The saloon's back door opened, and someone leaned out, calling, "Dad, you out there?" It was Jason's voice.

Sighing, Vidalia felt as if she'd been saved by the bell. God knew she was dreading the rest of what she had to confess to this man.

She got to her feet and turned toward the saloon.

He got up too, put his hands on her shoulders. "Oh, no. No, you're not getting off that easy." And he turned her to face him again. "Why, Vidalia? Why would you lie to me about that?"

"Dad?" Jason called.

"Why? Come on, Bobby Joe, I was a married woman. A mother of four. I'd committed adultery."

"No one ever would've known."

She lowered her head. "I thought about telling you then, but you said you were leaving town. And I just...I just thought it for the best to let you go."

He nodded, was silent for a long moment, during which his son called for him once more. "I wish I remembered," he said. "I've dreamed about being with you like that, so many times. To think I actually had it and was too damn drunk to remember...."

She lowered her head. "Do you hate me for not telling you?"

"I couldn't hate you if I tried." He hooked a finger under her chin, lifted her head, kissed her softly and sweetly, and then a little more deeply. When he lifted his lips from hers, he whispered, "I'd sure like another night like that with you, Vidalia."

"Ohhh, you're the devil in blue jeans, tempting me like that Bobby Joe McIntyre."

"I'm noting only that you didn't say no."

"I didn't say yes, either."

"Then I'm gonna keep on trying." He kissed her once more, then turning her, kept his arm around her. "But you said there was more."

"There is. But I think we'd best save it. We've got guests to entertain and your firstborn's not gonna stop bellering until we get back inside."

"You sure it can wait, Vidalia? It felt...important."

He was staring into her eyes as he asked the question. She

averted her gaze. "It's important," she admitted. "But one confession is enough for one night, don't you think, Bobby Joe?"

"I do, at that." He tightened his arm around her, pulling her closer to his side, and they walked together back to the saloon.

~

The next day morning, Bobby phoned to invite her to go Christmas shopping with him, and Vidalia was all too happy to oblige. They shopped all morning long. The man had shockingly deep pockets, and he didn't mind dipping into them. She helped him figure out what to get for two of his sons by asking him questions about the young men and guiding him from there. For example, Joey, the youngest, had a penchant for video games when he was younger, and they found him an actual arcade version of his favorite old video game. The thing was huge and would be delivered to the saloon the next day. Rob was into the outdoors, so for him, a hand crafted wooden canoe that was so beautiful it took even Vidalia's breath away. For Jason, they were drawing a blank, and had stopped for lunch to give their brains a rest. Their table was in the food court in the middle of the closest mall, a full hour from home. Holiday music was playing, and the place was decked to the rafters with tinsel and garland, glittery stars and snowflakes. In the distance, a half circle of twinkling trees bordered a jolly old man in a red suit, who sat in a throne-like chair in front of a mile-long line of eager children with wonder in their eyes.

"I wish I'd been around more when my kids were growing up," Bobby mused. "I was gone so much."

"I know. You've told me. But regrets are a waste of time. And you're making it up to them right now."

"How do your girls feel about their...father, now?"

Why did he hesitate before saying the word "father?" Did he know? Or suspect? She pushed the thought aside. She was going to tell him. It was just a matter of choosing her moment. "It's a different situation, Bobby Joe. He died before he could even try to apologize to them, much less make things right the way you're doing now with your boys."

"Still," he said. "I'd like to know."

She shrugged. "We don't talk about him a lot. I think they might still resent that he wasn't there for them. But they also know that he couldn't be other than who he was. You can't hate someone for being who they are. I've raised them to know that. And the truth of the matter is, when you know better, you do better. Sadly, he died before he got around to knowing a better way. I think he knows now."

That comment made him look up swiftly. "You think he...went to heaven? Even with everything he did? Bigamy?"

"I *know* he went to heaven, Bobby Joe. I've had extensive conversations about this with Reverend Jackson, who you still need to meet, by the way, and with Selene as well."

He frowned. "Why Selene?"

"She's...spiritual. Deep. Sometimes the things that girl spews sound like they're coming from a hundred year old prophet just out of his cave. She's a special one, she is."

He nodded, leaning forward, having forgotten his sandwich and cup of soup. She pointed at it so he'd continue eating. He'd lost a little weight, she thought, since he'd been in town.

He ate, and she talked. "Selene doesn't believe in an actual Hell. She says if God is love, then a place of eternal torment isn't impossible. And that makes sense to me."

He washed a bite of his sandwich down with a drink of sweet tea. "I'm sure your Reverend Jackson doesn't agree with her."

"Don't be so sure. He says it's a dilemma that's always troubled him too, for the very same reasons. And that he thinks some things won't make any sense until we cross over, and that we just have to trust that all is well until then."

"What do you think happens?" he asked her.

She held his eyes, and her heart ached for the secrets he was keeping, and the worry in her own mind. "I think maybe when we get to the other side, we look back on our deeds, both good and bad, and we see the lessons in all of it. I think we get wiser, and that we heal."

"That's a beautiful way to look at things."

She nodded. "And if I'm wrong, I'll find out when I cross over."

He smiled, dipping the final corner of his sandwich into the bit of soup he had left in his bowl. "I guess we all will," he said softly. And he seemed a little bit grim just then.

Vidalia reached across the table and covered her hand with his. "What's wrong, Bobby? Sometimes you look so sad it breaks my heart."

He met her eyes, unashamed of the moisture that had come into his own. None spilled over. He blinked it away. "I don't want to tell you yet. Not yet, Vidalia. Don't make me. We're having so much fun together. And it's Christmas."

Those words sent a shiver down her spine. So it *was* something bad. Way down deep, her suspicion took on more substance, but she refused to look at it or even acknowledge that it was there.

"After the holiday?"

He nodded.

"Right after?"

Again he nodded. "I know it's not fair, my keeping my secret and choosing my time to share it. And in the very next breath, asking you to reveal the rest of yours. But I am. I have to."

She drew her hands back suddenly and looked down at the table. "Bobby, I–"

"Is Selene my daughter?"

Vidalia slammed her eyes closed, like slamming a door on the secret she had kept for far too long. But it was too late. It was already out. She drew a deep breath, prayed for strength and forced herself to look him in the eye. "I was going to tell you last night. And I've been working up to it all morning. The truth is, Bobby, she might be. But I don't know for sure."

"How can you not know?"

She held up a hand to ask him for patience. "John came home only a couple of days after you...after we....after you left. It was six weeks later I realized I was carrying Selene. You were long gone and I hadn't heard a word. I was mortified and ashamed of myself for cheating on my husband, and I just...I saw no good that could come from digging around in any of it. I just never looked into it any further." She lowered her head. "To tell you the truth, I was afraid to."

He sighed heavily. "You should've told me, Vidalia. I had a right to know."

"I don't deny that. I was wrong, and I'm sorry. But I want you to ask yourself what difference it would have made if you had known? You were as much as an absentee father to your boys as my husband was to my girls."

"No. Not quite that much," he denied.

She nodded, unwilling to argue the point. He was right. At least he hadn't had another wife, another family, competing for his attention. "All right, not quite that much. But still, it wasn't like you would've spent time with her, raised her as your own. Not back then. You were all wrapped up in making your fortune."

He was silent for a long moment, and then, at last, he heaved a heavy sigh. "You're right. But I'd have...at least tried to help you support her. I would've sent money—"

"And I'd have sent it back. I'm a proud woman, Bobby Joe. One of the things I'm proudest of is having raised those five girls on my own. I wouldn't have taken your money. If I had, they wouldn't have turned out to be the women they are, and I'm damn proud of the women they are."

He nodded. "You should be."

She looked at her sandwich, half-eaten, and pushed the plate away. "I've never told Selene. But if you want me to, you have a right to ask that of me, I suppose. Or if you want some kind of testing done to be sure—"

"I don't know if I need to tell her or not. I...I need to mull on this a little. It's a lot to take in."

Nodding, Vidalia pushed away from the table, picking up her tray and heading for the nearest wastebasket. Bobby came behind her, put his hands on her shoulders. "I'm not angry with you, Vidalia."

"You should be," she said. "I deserve your anger. This has been eating at me all this time. I was so wrong—"

"You were a single mother, for all intents and purposes, and you had to put that first. I don't blame you at all for making the decision you did."

She set the now empty tray atop the stack of others and turned to face him. "I did wrong, Bobby, and I had every intention of telling you the truth today. I was...working up my courage. But I readily admit that I am desperately in need of your forgiveness."

"I don't see that there's anything to forgive—"

"I need it. And I need you to mean it. So give it some time to settle in, and really think it over, Bobby Joe. This is a stain I've been wearing on my soul for a long time, and you're the only one who can remove it."

He nodded, leaned down, kissed her forehead. "I forgive you, Vidalia. And I mean it. I'm not gonna change my mind, even if I think on it for a few years. And I'll tell you why." He licked his lips, lowered his forehead and pressed it to hers. "It's because I love you."

"Oh, Lord, Bobby Joe, it's too soon to be saying such—"

"Too soon? I've loved you for more than twenty years, woman. Listen, I'm a man who knows his own mind. His own heart. At least, I am now. I've made a vow to say what I feel to everyone in my life, right at the moment I have the chance, because life is short, Vidalia, and you just never know when you'll get another shot. I love you. I've loved you since I came to work for you a hundred years ago. And I'll love you till the day I...." He stopped there and swallowed hard.

And then he smiled quite suddenly and said, "A ventriloquist's doll!"

Vidalia frowned, blinking up at him in complete confusion.

"That's the one Christmas present Jason ever asked for that I didn't get him. He got on this kick after seeing an old TV show on a Sunday afternoon that featured Edgar Bergen and his Charlie McCarthy puppet. I looked everywhere. But there were none to be found."

"Well, why don't you use that fancy phone of yours to track one down?" she asked. "If you can't find one on the Internet, then one doesn't exist." She was glad the subject had lightened up so much. And grateful that he wasn't furious with her for the secret she had kept all these years. If only she knew for sure, and if only she could have the courage to tell Selene the truth. But there was one thing Vidalia Brand feared more than she feared the devil himself, and that was losing the love of her daughters. What if they hated her for what she had done? What if they lost respect for her?

And she was worried about more than that, too. Because that niggling little theory about this secret Bobby Joe was keeping from her was growing bigger all the time, and she didn't like where it was leading her.

God was punishing her, that's what it was. She was being punished for the sin she'd committed and then compounded by the lie she had told.

~

Bobby Joe found the doll on Ebay, and rather than trusting overnight shipping this close to the holiday, decided to make the drive to get it himself, right then. Vidalia had the saloon to run and had already lost a night's business by helping him with his, so he took her home first and made the drive on his own.

And as he drove, he kept putting Selene's pretty face in his mind, and searching it for similarities to his own and to his sons. Remarkably, he saw plenty, at least in his imagination. In fact, that baby photo he'd glimpsed in the ornament the night they'd decorated the tree had looked an awful lot like one of Joey's baby pictures.

While he was out, he would use the opportunity to find gifts for Selene and her sisters as well. And for Vidalia's grandkids. And for Vidalia.

What could he possibly give to her?

Oh, he had a solid idea about that. But what he had in mind was something it would be unfair to give her until he'd told her the truth. Because it came with a question she could not possibly answer until she had all the information at hand. And yet, he bought it anyway. Took him the better part of an hour to pick it out, too. But as soon as he saw it, he knew it was right.

The small golden hued diamond formed the center of a daisy that was surrounded by brilliant white diamonds in the shape of its petals. Daisies had always been Vidalia's favorite flower.

Now all he needed to do was figure out how and when to tell her the truth. And how to ask her to be his wife for whatever time he had left.

CHAPTER EIGHT

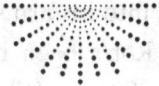

"*H*ello, Bobby?" Why Vidalia's throat felt full of sand, she could only guess. Nervous as a prom date. At her age.

"Hey, Vidalia. Happy Christmas Eve." He sounded...off. Tired or something. "Didn't expect to hear from you this morning."

"I hope I'm not calling too early."

"If I could start every day hearing that sultry voice of yours, I'd be a happy man. And it can never be too early. Or too late. I hope."

His flattery could've distracted her and might have, had she been a twenty-year-old. But she was old enough and wise enough and paying enough attention to hear behind the words. "Are you all right, Bobby? You sound odd. You're not sick or anything–"

"It would be pretty lousy of me to get sick on Christmas Eve, wouldn't it now?" He laughed and forced–she thought–more lightness into his voice. "Don't you worry about me, Vidalia. I'm gonna have the holiday of a lifetime. Now why don't you tell me what's on your mind."

She smiled a little, despite the nagging worry that wouldn't quite go away. "I was thinking that Christmas Day is gonna be bustling with your boys, my girls, their kids and their hubbies and whoever else shows up. Your boys have any women in their lives, Bobby Joe?"

"Besides their mother, no. Joey's determined to stay free and easy as long as possible. Jason seems to be waiting for the perfect female to just fall into his arms, but isn't very proactive about finding her. And Rob's been burned badly and hasn't healed enough to try again just yet. Why do you ask?"

She shrugged. "I was just thinking about the Haggerty sisters."

"Why is that name familiar?"

"It's the restaurant where we had lunch, over in Tucker Lake. It's owned by five gorgeous sisters, all of whom are still single, and their grandmother, a woman I've always admired."

"Betty Jean. I remember you talking with her."

"Should I invite them to join us for something over the holidays? Maybe take Rob's mind off his wounded heart?

"No. I mean...just no. I don't think my boys would be even a little bit appreciative. And if they acted ungrateful I'd have to show them I could still kick their keisters. Not something I really want to do at holiday time."

She smiled. He was sounding more like himself. Teasing and light. She could hear his smile in his voice, see the sparkle in his blue, blue eyes. "Well, that's not what I was calling about anyway. I'm gonna be shockingly forward with you here, Bobby Joe, but um...I think we should have a Christmas for just the two of us."

"Instead of–"

"No. I don't ever do anything instead of my family. I was thinking in addition to. And I was thinking tonight would be the perfect time. Everyone else is busy with their last minute planning and baking and wrapping. The night before Christmas has been the quietest night of the year around my house since the last of those girls got married and moved out."

His breath whispered into the phone. She imagined she felt its warmth caressing her ear. "That sounds a little sad, Vidalia."

"Oh, no. Not sad at all. I turn off all the lights except for the ones on my Christmas tree. I put on soft holiday music and light candles. I pour myself a special drink and sit in the living room breathing in the pine and I kind of...reflect on the year gone by. Sometimes on the whole lifetime gone by. And to tell you the truth, Bobby Joe, there hasn't been a single Christmas Eve that you haven't been a part of that reflection."

"You don't say." His voice sounded a little softer, maybe a little gruff too.

She shrugged as if he could see her. "It would be nice to have you actually here with me, instead of just whispering like a ghost through my mind."

"I'll be there. What can I bring?"

"Yourself. And my present. You did get me a present, didn't you?" She had absolutely no doubt that he had, or she wouldn't have asked. She'd got him something as well.

"You'll just have to wait and see. What time should I arrive, sweet Vidalia?"

"Seven, if you can stand to wait for your dinner that long."

"You don't have to cook for me."

"Shush now. You just show up at seven, all right?"

"I will. I don't know how I'm gonna wait that long, but—"

"It's only eleven hours. That's not so much more waiting, not after all these years. Besides, I have to get ready." She hung up the phone before her suddenly tremulous vocal chords gave her away. Nervous as a prom date.

She went to her bedroom after that, opened her closets and stared in almost blindly. She even moved hangers around, and took a few things out, holding them in front of her and turning to face the mirror attached to her antique dresser.

And then she looked a little harder and moved a little closer, tipping her head to one side and seeing the lines at the corners of her eyes in a way she'd never seen them before. They'd been there. It wasn't that she was unaware of them. If she looked closely, she could see the beginnings of lines across her forehead, too. Not deep, barely there, even. More like coming attractions. Her lashes and brows weren't as lush and abundant as they had once been. Her lips, not as full. And she didn't need to take off her clothes to remind her that her breasts were no longer as perky as they had been in her youth. Her waist, not as tiny, her tummy, not as flat. Her hips were wider, curving out from her waist.

"Mom? You up here?"

She grunted a reply and leaned nearer the mirror.

"Mom?" Maya was at the bedroom door, coming inside, taking in the clothes on the bed, and her mother's close self-scrutiny, no doubt. "What's going on, Mom?"

"I'm aging," Vidalia said.

"You sound surprised."

Tearing her gaze from the mirror, she managed to turn and face her firstborn. "I guess I shouldn't be. I just haven't been paying that much attention."

"Mom, you're fif–"

"I know how old I am. I just...didn't know I looked it." The mirror pulled her back until Maya stood beside her, leaning just as close, looking just as intently at their reflections.

"You don't look your age. You look my age. I have more crow's feet than you do."

"Pssh," Vidalia replied.

"I don't think it's that you never noticed before. I think it's that you never cared before. What's going on, Mom? Is it Bobby Joe?"

Vidalia had never been much for vanity. What the heck was getting into her? Sighing, she turned from the mirror and looked at her daughter. "Yes, it's Bobby Joe. I um...." She looked at the floor. "I'm in love with him."

Maya gasped. It was a soft sound, a surprised one, and Vidalia couldn't quite meet her eyes. She just kept looking down. "I don't think I realized it myself until just now, but the truth is, I've been in love with him for as long as I've known him. But things were....well, you know. Impossible then."

"I had no idea," Maya whispered.

"I'm going to tell him so. Tonight. I thought we could have Christmas Eve together, just the two of us, but-" She waved a hand, sort of indicating the clothes on the bed and the danged mirror all in one gesture.

"Oh, Mama. Oh, come here."

Vidalia looked up with a frown, glimpsing tears on her daughter's cheeks just before she found herself enveloped in a hug. "Well, you don't need to be so emotional about it, daughter. It's just-"

"I've wished this for you a thousand times," Maya told her. "Maybe a million. We all have." Sniffling, she stood back, hands on her mother's shoulders, wet eyes meeting hers. "You just relax. I'm gonna call Edie and Kara and-"

"No. No, wait, this isn't big announcement time or family meeting time, it's just-"

"It's just, let's help Mom get ready for her romantic evening time. C'mon Mama. We owe you this. Let us help."

She pursed her lips, glanced at the mirror again, and nodded. "To tell you the truth, I'd be lost without you. He's important to me. And you're important to me, and it just doesn't seem right that those two things shouldn't be all bundled up together."

Maya grinned, dashed away her tears, and pulled out her cellphone. And Vidalia wondered if the enormity of the guilt on her shoulders could grow any larger. What would they think of her when they learned the truth?

~

Bobby Joe felt like a million bucks. If he didn't know better, he'd have thought he was in the peak of health as he got ready for his evening with Vidalia. He put the ring in his pocket. He couldn't ask her until he told her the truth, of course, and he really didn't want to tell her the truth until after Christmas, because it would ruin her holiday. But he didn't know how things were going to go tonight, and he wanted to be prepared for anything.

He dressed nice. Wore a suit that accentuated his shape, which was still damn good, if he did say so himself. He added a bolo tie, because he thought she'd like that. And when he arrived, he didn't show up empty handed. He brought a bottle of the best brandy he had—top-shelf stuff, remembering that she'd liked it—and a bouquet of Daisies he'd had to order from a town two hours away. It was not daisy season. But it was worth it when he saw them. Pretty white petals, around bright yellow centers, with fine mists of tiny blue forget me nots all in between.

He felt oddly nervous when he stood at her garland decked front door, facing a giant wreath, with his flowers in one hand, preparing to knock. He could smell whatever was cooking from outside, and it made his stomach rumble.

And then she opened the door, and he forgot everything else. She'd turned herself into a movie star, he thought. Makeup— just a little, but somehow it made her eyes sparkle and shine even more than usual, lined in black that way. And her hair, her riotous curls had been tamed into a long, sleek, gleaming style. She wore a long dress with a plunging neckline that showed off her lush cleavage, and a sparkling necklace of crystal snowflakes. And there was a slit up one side that showed peeks of thigh and made him tremble.

He released a long, slow whistle as his eyes devoured the high heeled, open toed shoes, and made their way back up to her face again. "Just when I didn't think you could get any prettier. I guess you can gild a lily after all."

She smiled, apparently approving of the compliment. "You're not so bad yourself. Those boots make you almost too tall for me."

"Then I'll take 'em off," he said as he stepped inside, handing her the flowers and the brandy. "Two of your favorites, as I recall."

"Thank you, Bobby Joe. You've got a good memory."

"Not as good as I wish it was." He winked at her.

She blushed, turning away to hide it and going to the sink for a vase and some water. She arranged the flowers, and unable to wait, he walked up behind her, put his hands on her shoulders. She bent her head sideways to run her soft cheek over one of those hands, and he thought he was the luckiest man alive, right now, tonight.

Setting the vase full of flowers aside, she turned in his arms, twisted hers around his neck, and standing up on tiptoe, kissed him in a way that whispered promises he knew better than to expect her to keep.

Then lowering down again, leaving his heart pounding like the hind foot of an alarmed jack rabbit, she turned and walked away. "Dinner's ready. I thought we'd eat in front of the fireplace."

"I thought I caught a whiff of wood smoke. That'll be nice, Vidalia. Here, let me get that." She was bending over the oven, removing two dinner plates, already loaded with food, and he waited until she straightened up to make his offer, because he was distracted by the view. He was polite, but he wasn't crazy.

He took the plates from her, pot holders and all, and she

said, "Go on in. I'll get drinks. Wine with dinner okay with you?"

"And brandy with dessert," he said.

She got wine glasses down while he carried their meals into the living room, and then he stood there for a moment, taking it all in. He'd had houses. Big ones that could be called mansions, though he hated the term. Smaller ones too, vacation places he bought and sold as the whim took him. There had been a beach house on the Gulf and a summer place up in the mountains of Tennessee that he'd kept but hadn't visited in ages. He'd had a great big stately plantation style house in Dallas. Judith got that in the divorce. After that he'd moved into a modern architectural wonder with uneven peaks and as much glass as wood.

But this wasn't a just house. This was a home. The living room was wide and warm. The furniture was arranged so it all sort of faced each other and the fireplace and the Christmas tree that stood in the corner to the right of it. The sofa was huge and soft, and it had a twin. Two double width recliners had been squeezed in there as well. He supposed with a family as big as hers, there needed to be plenty of places to sit. He went to one of the dual recliners, because the coffee table was in front of it, already set with a red and green checked cloth napkins with napkin rings that looked like holiday wreaths holding them, two sets of silverware already laid out, and tall glasses of ice water too.

He set the plates down, waiting for her to sit before he did. Then he joined her, nodding in appreciation as he did. That tree of hers had so many homemade ornaments there was hardly room for the few store-bought ones she'd added. Popsicle stick and yarn God's eyes in every color combination you could think of. Tiny pewter frames with newborns all pink and wrinkly held within. Styrofoam balls lovingly painted by tiny hands. Pine cones dipped in glue, then rolled in glitter, dangling from strings. Every Christmas project of five young women and three grandkids decked that tree, and he thought it was the prettiest thing he'd ever seen, next to Vidalia herself.

"You like my ragtag mishmash of ornaments?" she asked.

He nodded. "I love it." And I love you, he thought, but he didn't say it just then. He didn't want to keep putting pressure on her to reply in kind, and he thought every time he said it, that was probably what he was doing, intentionally or not.

The fireplace was brick, and three stockings hung from it, each with a different name spelled out in glitter. The grandkids. Tyler, Dahlia and CC.

Behind them the fire snapped and cracked and filled the room with warmth and holiday cheer. And the entire mantle was lined with holiday decorations, trees and Santas, a sleigh and reindeer, photos of the kids on Santa's knee.

As he turned his attention to the plate of food in front of him, which included a T-bone steak that had apparently been sawed off a T-Rex, a baked potato already loaded with melting sour cream, a slice of warm homemade bread melting with butter, a mound of asparagus, and some glazed carrots, he wondered how he was going to eat it all.

"Don't even start," Vidalia said. "You've lost weight just since you've been here."

"Have I?"

"Yeah, and you need to put some back on if you want me to be seen in public with you. I'm not going to walk around next to a guy who makes me feel chubby."

"You are voluptuous. There's a difference."

"And I intend to stay that way. So since I'm not gonna skinny down, you're gonna have to chub up." She winked at him, and he forced a smile he didn't feel.

He wasn't going to gain any weight, and he probably wasn't going to be able to do this fabulous meal of hers justice. The symptoms of the end didn't come on until things were about to get very bad, very fast, or so his doctors had told him. And they had begun. He was nearly out of time, then. But he was sure as hell going to try to make it through the holiday.

He sawed off a piece of steak, so tender he didn't really even need the knife. Vidalia picked up a remote, thumbed a button, and soft romantic holiday music came on. She leaned against him a little, then sat up and dug into her own meal.

He surprised himself with how much he managed to tuck away, but had to plead for mercy where dessert was concerned. She agreed to put it off until later, then excused herself to use the restroom.

He took the opportunity to clear away their dishes, rinse them and load them into the dishwasher. When she came back, he took his turn freshening up. He'd even brought along a toothbrush, that was how hopeful he was that there would be some making out going on tonight. The kind that would make a teenager blush.

If he could hold up. He was tired. Weaker than normal. It wasn't a good sign.

When he returned to the living room, he held out a hand instead of joining her on the couch. She took it, and he pulled her to her feet and then right up against him, and he started moving her around to the music. *Merry Christmas, Baby* wasn't the easiest to dance to, but he thought they did a pretty good job. God, she felt so good against his chest. And her hair smelled good, too.

She looked up at him, smiling. "I thought maybe I could give you your Christmas present tonight," she whispered.

"I've got no objections."

"It's got two parts to it." She snuggled her head onto his chest. He closed his eyes and hoped the next song would be just as slow and mellow. So far, they all had been. Maybe she'd planned it that way.

"I didn't see anything under the tree."

"Well, it's not the kind of gift you can wrap," she said, very softly. And maybe her voice trembled a little bit. "You'll get one of those tomorrow."

"This is getting mighty interesting now," he said. "Go on...?"

"Well, the first part of it is this." She lifted up her head, and looked right up into his eyes. "I love you, too."

Everything in his life lit up. *She* lit up. She glowed momentarily with backlighting that seemed to be a mixture of gold and red and white around the outside. He stared down at her, blinking in blatant disbelief.

"I think I've always loved you. And I have no doubt that I always will."

He opened his mouth to tell her how much that meant to him. How long he'd been waiting, how much he'd been hoping, and how sorry he was that their time together would have to be so brief.

But he found he couldn't speak. Something odd was happening and he felt like he wasn't in control of his body anymore. He thought the music had changed. It sounded like a choir of about a thousand voices, all singing different notes, but in perfect harmony, no words, just that tone. And the room around Vidalia had sort of vanished. There was only her, all lit up like the angel on top of the tree, looking up at him, and saying, "Bobby Joe? Honey, can you hear me?"

"You love me," he said. And smiled. That smile stayed in place, even when his eyes fell closed and his body fell off him, just as if he'd stepped out of it. As if it was a suit of clothes, just falling bonelessly to the floor, while he remained up above.

But then Vidalia fell to the floor too, bending over that discarded suit and shaking it, and calling his name, and starting to cry.

"I'm not there. I'm up here," he tried to say, and he noticed the body on the floor. The way the mouth moved when he tried to speak, and that was when it hit him that he had left his body.

Was this it, then? Was he dead? No, not yet! Please, not yet!

The ring, he had to give her the ring. He stared down at the body on the floor, willed the hand to move, strained every part of whatever he was now, and by gosh, it worked. That hand moved. It didn't feel like he was moving it directly. More like he was the puppeteer, pulling the strings.

Vidalia crawled away from him, but only a few feet, grabbing a phone, then hurrying back again. She dialed, spoke rapidly, and clicked off while he could still hear the operator telling her to stay on the line. Her second call was to one of her daughters. He didn't know which one. He heard her say, "Call your sisters. Call his sons. Meet us at the hospital. It's bad, I just know it."

She dropped the phone, bending over his body, close to his face. "Bobby Joe, dammit, I knew something was wrong. You should've told me. Come on, don't give up. Hang on for me, will you?"

He wanted to nod, but every asset was focused on moving the hand. He closed it around the box in his pocket. He couldn't feel the box with his hand, he could just tell that there was something between the fingers and the palm, and he willed them to squeeze hold of it as he tried to tug the hand back out.

Frowning, she looked down, apparently feeling the movement.

She took his wrist, gently pulling his hand from his pocket. Yes, finally! He relaxed the hand open, letting go of all that effort and floating more easily and lightly above his body. The little box fell out of that pale, lifeless hand that did not feel like his own, rolling onto the carpet, and Vidalia gasped softly. "Oh, Bobby Joe, you didn't...."

He wanted to watch her open it, to see her expression when she did, but there was noise out front. Time sure had passed quickly, or someone had been close by.

"Mama!"

One of the girls. He didn't know which one. There was something pulling him away, something so beautiful that he

116

couldn't focus much on what was going on below. The choir grew louder, and he turned his attention toward it and saw swirls of color that didn't exist on earth. They were outside the spectrum.

Wow. That was something. *Are you seeing this, Vidalia? Are you seeing this?*

CHAPTER NINE

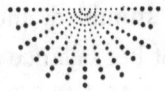

"*M*ama, what happened?"

"Maya," Caleb said, "keep the kids in the kitchen, hon. Let me try to help." Caleb knelt beside Bobby Joe, opposite Vidalia, but she only barely noticed him there, and his voice faded to a sort of deep hum.

Don't take him from me, Lord. It's too soon.

The front door opened and banged shut again. And then again every few heartbeats or so, and more voices joined the insect-like drone that was filling her head as she stared down at him. *So pale. And thinner than I even realized. Look at his collarbones.*

Noticing his collarbones made her notice that someone had opened his shirt, and she dragged her eyes off Bobby's sweet face long enough to look to see who. Paramedics...efficient and confident, and asking her to move aside and let them work. Who knew how long they'd been asking? She'd only just noticed they were here. Numbly, she told herself to move out of the way, but her eyes locked on Bobby's face again, and her hands tightened on the one they held, and for the life of her she just couldn't back away.

"Bobby, don't go," she whispered. "Bobby, don't you go." His eyes were closed, his lips as soft as they'd been when he'd been kissing her only a few minutes ago. She looked at his nose, at his jaw, at his eyebrows, memorizing him in her heart.

"Mama, come on. Let them help him, Mama," said two of her daughters at once. Their hands were on her shoulders.

Nodding, she laid Bobby's hand on his chest, and tried to get up onto her feet, but she stumbled, and one of her strong sons in law caught her. She got her balance as Alex helped her a few steps away, and then she looked up and all her girls were standing there, wide, wet eyes so full of love for her that it broke the log jam, and she just burst into tears.

"Did someone call his sons?" she asked, knowing she'd asked before, but she couldn't remember the answer. They were walking across the blacktop lot toward the glass doors of the hospital. Only a short distance away, the ambulance sat outside the emergency room doors, having beat them here, but not by much.

"They're already here," Selene said. "That's Jason's truck, next to where we parked."

"Oh." She nodded, wanting to go directly to the ER doors. Only her family all around her, herding her with them to the approved entrance, kept her from going. They got inside, and while some of them veered toward the nurses' desk, she just kept walking, aiming in the direction of the ER. And Bobby.

Her family came behind her, every last one of them. She didn't know who'd been the last minute babysitter, but someone must have come through.

Jason came out of nowhere and said, "Vidalia. Good. You're here."

"I'm here. Where is he? What have they said?"

"Nothing. Nothing, but as I was just about to tell my brothers..." he turned to look behind him, and Vidalia realized there was a waiting room behind there. He hadn't come out of nowhere, he'd come out of there. Joey and Rob were standing within, pale and shocky looking. There were orange vinyl chairs mounted to the walls, and two rows down the middle, bolted to the floor. There were vending machines with junk food and junk drinks. The only healthy thing in the hospital waiting room was the bottled water, and she wasn't so sure about that.

She nodded hello to each of the boys, when what she wanted to do was hug them. But they weren't close enough for that, were they?

Her question was answered when Joey came and hugged her. "Vidalia, are you okay?"

Behind him, Rob looked her over worriedly. "They said he was with you when he collapsed."

"And Jason was about to tell us something about that. He got as far as...'Dad's sick.'" This, Joey said with a look over her head toward his oldest brother, who had come back into the waiting room on the tide of her family.

Vidalia turned too, sinking into a chair because her knees were too watery to hold her up any longer. "I knew it. I knew something was wrong with him. What is it Jason?"

Jason stayed standing, though everyone else sat. "It's a blood condition. He's known for three months now."

Joey and Rob looked at each other and then at Jason again.

Vidalia said, "He's known what, exactly, for three months now, Jason?"

Jason lowered his head and swallowed hard. "That's he's dying."

"God no," she whispered.

"How long have you known?" Joey asked softly.

"Since I got here."

"And you didn't tell us?" Robb demanded. "How could you not—"

"He wanted to give you a Christmas to remember," Vidalia interrupted. She met Jason's eyes. "That's it, isn't it? He was going to tell us all right after the holiday. But he didn't want that news to ruin it. He wanted us all to have one wonderful, perfect family Christmas with him."

"Almost word for word what he said to me," Jason said, wiping a tear away from the corner of his eye before it could spill over.

"So this is...this is it? His time is up?" Vidalia asked.

"This fits what the doctors told him."

Vidalia lowered her head, her girls were all around her, hugging her, touching her, holding her, patting her.

The ER doors opened and a grim faced doctor she didn't know—she'd have so preferred someone she knew—came to stand among them. "He's stable for now. We've got him settled in a room, and he's comfortable."

"I just can't believe there's no cure for him, Doctor," Vidalia said. "He's got more money than God. Surely somewhere in the world there's a cure for this—"

"There *is* a cure, ma'am. He needs a bone marrow transplant, but he's got a rare blood type and none of his sons are matches. He's on the waiting list, but I'm afraid he's run out of time."

That buzzing sound came into her head again, and she heard nothing else. Nothing at all as she stood there with her gaze turned inward. And when she focused outward again they were all staring at her, and Selene stood closest of all. Searching her mother's eyes, she said, "I have a rare blood type too, or so they tell me every time I give a pint. You should test me. Shouldn't they, Mom?"

Vidalia met Selene's eyes.

"I can do math, you know," Selene said. "And I look a little like Joey."

Vidalia could feel the realization of what Selene was talking about blinking into each person's head in that waiting room. Her girls were looking at her in shock, and Bobby's sons were staring at her in dawning realization, as well.

"Yes," Vidalia said, nodding slowly. "Yes, Bobby and I had...one night together all those years ago, and yes, there's a very good chance that was the night Selene was conceived. I was married, I was lonely, I was drunk, and.... No. No, you know what? I was in love. That's what I was. I was in love with the man I was meant to be with. And I couldn't be with him, and that was the tragedy. Not the affair. Not the pregnancy. Not even the lie I've told all this time. The tragedy is that we were meant to be together and we couldn't be, and now we can be and he's...he's–"

"He's found a donor," Selene said softly. "I know it. I can feel it." Turning, she kissed her husband hard. "I love you, Cory. And I've gotta do this."

"I know you do. I'll call your friends, get them to fire up their cauldrons. I know the deal."

She smiled, and turned to the doctor. "Take me to the bone marrow drilling rig, Doc. It doesn't sound like we have time to waste."

The doctor looked befuddled, but seemed to be getting it. Before he could lead her away, Joey shot forward and hugged Selene hard. "I have a sister," he said, sort of into her hair, but everyone heard it.

She seemed startled at first, but then she softened and hugged him back. "I always wanted a big brother," she said, looking him in the eye, then past him at the other two. "Looks I got three of them now."

Vidalia's paralysis broke as her youngest pushed through the double doors, and she lunged forward, caught Selene's shoulders, and held on. "Honey, wait. You don't have to do this. To risk–"

"I'm doing it, Mom." She smiled broadly, kissed Vidlia's cheek. "Merry Christmas." Then she looked back at her four sisters and stuck out her tongue. "Top that, bitches." She winked and sashayed through the double doors that closed behind her.

Vidalia sat down, suddenly aware that everyone in this room now knew the secret she'd been so afraid of for so long. They all knew she'd been unfaithful to her husband. They all knew she'd sinned, given birth to another man's child and lied about it. They all knew she wasn't perfect.

Melusine pressed a styrofoam mug of cocoa into her hand and sank into the chair beside her. Edie sat in the one on other side, leaning on her shoulder. Maya and Kara knelt in front of her, holding her hands. "It's okay, Mama," Maya said.

"It was such a long time ago," Kara added.

"And our father had kids by two other women," Mel said.

"That we know of," Edie added. "And he was secretly married to one of them."

"It's really okay, Mom. We love you. Nothing's changed," Maya said.

"Something's changed," Mel said. "We know you're human now, like the rest of us. Frankly, I like you better with a few flaws."

"And it explains a helluva lot about Selene," Kara said.

"Really. I thought she was left by Gypsies, not McIntyres," Edie added, and they all laughed.

Vidalia sighed, and a good deal of the tension that had been pulling at her back and shoulders melted away. She looked toward the ER doors and waited, and prayed.

Then, remembering, she dipped her hand into her pocket, where she'd dropped the small black velvet box Bobby Joe had worked so hard to fish out as he lay there on her living room floor. She had a pretty good notion what was inside, and it made her throat tighten till it was hard to breathe past her tears.

She wasn't going to open it and look inside. She was going to wait for Bobby to show it to her himself. Until then, she needed a little one-on-one time with the Lord.

"I need to find out if this place has a chapel," she whispered.

"I'll find out, Vi," Cory said softly, and he went to the nurse's desk to ask.

~

Vidalia knelt in the hospital chapel in front of a stand with a statue of Jesus, who looked down at her with his serene, wise eyes. There were other statues, symbols of other faiths all around this room. But Jesus was her guy. Always had been.

She knelt in front of Him, bowed her head, folded her hands, and let her tears flow. She couldn't talk. Not for a long, long time. But her sobs seemed to dissipate when she heard, off in the distance, a clock striking the hour. On and on it struck. Midnight.

She blinked her eyes dry. "It's Christmas. It's the perfect time for a miracle. Oh, I know, Lord, I know—I was wrong to keep this secret. And now to find out that telling it was the only way to save him. Could've saved him long before now, too. Oh, please don't let it be too late. Please let it be in time. I am a good woman, Lord. I am not a perfect woman, but I am a good woman. I've never asked you for much. For anything really, at least not for myself. I deserve this. You make sure my Selene is okay through this, Lord. And if you can find it in your heart, let Bobby and me have our time together. And when you have to call us home, call us home together, too. We've spent way too much time apart. You made us for each other, after all. I'm just sorry it took us so long to realize it."

A car passed by outside, and the headlights blinded her. But as they faded, their light passed slowly over the face of the statue. And for the barest moment, she could've sworn He'd smiled at her as, from the distance, church bells rang in Christmas.

~

"Mama!"

Vidalia didn't turn at the sound of Kara's voice in the chapel doorway. She stayed perfectly still, and maybe braced herself a little for what was to come next.

"Mama, you have to come."

Blinking away her tears, she took a deep breath. "Thy will be done," she whispered. "Amen." Then she got to her feet and was surprised how hard it was to straighten her legs. She'd been kneeling there far longer than she had known.

Kara put an arm around her shoulders, holding her close and walking her out of the chapel and through the hospital corridors. When they reached the waiting room, Edie came to her other side, also holding her, and Mel and Maya crowded close too. "A nurse said to gather everyone. Said the doctor would be out to talk to us momentarily," Maya whispered.

"She didn't say anything else?" Vidalia searched the eyes of each of her daughters, but they all just shook their heads.

A small group of people passed by, carolers, all dressed in Victorian garb and carrying songbooks and looking a bit lost. Vidalia barely noticed them because the doctor came out through those double doors then and met her eyes.

"They both came through the surgery just fine," he said, smiling a little. "Your daughter is a strong woman, Mrs. Brand. She's already in recovery and arguing with the nurses."

"I'll go calm her down," she said, softly.

"You're not allowed–"

"In the recovery room. I know. I've broken that rule anytime one of my brood has been in there, and you'd better believe I'll

126

be breaking it again momentarily. Now tell me, doctor, Selene is fine, thank you Lord. How is Bobby?"

The surgeon's exasperated smile turned more serious. "Bobby's condition was pretty serious going in. He was weak. But the transplant should stop his disease from progressing any further. And in a few days, when Selene's marrow starts producing healthy new cells in him, we're gonna see rapid improvement. Right now, he's still critical. Keeping him alive long enough for those cells to do their work is our mission now."

She sniffled a little, nodded hard. "I'll go into that recovery room now."

"You're really not supposed to—"

"There's no point, Doc. She's going," Maya said.

"Might as well lead me to a sterile gown, one of those hideous hats, a mask, some gloves. And don't forget those bootie things to go over my shoes." The doc blinked at her, but she reached out a hand and clutched his arm. "And Doctor, thank you. Thank you more than I can ever say."

"Merry Christmas, Miz Brand."

"So far, it's just that. Let's hope it continues to be."

Vidalia walked into the recovery room to see Selene, standing beside a patient's bed, muttering something softly under her breath. A charm, a prayer, a healing rite...she didn't know which, but she appreciated it, whatever it was. A nurse was heading her way, stern eyed, but Vidalia picked up the pace and stepped into her path. "Leave her be," she said. "I've got this."

"She shouldn't be up—"

"It's Christmas. That's her...that's her father. You let it be."

The nurse seemed to hesitate, but then sighed and threw her hands in the air, turning and walking dramatically away. Smiling, Vidalia went to stand by Selene's side, slipping an arm around her middle.

"We sure do have some mighty big Christmases in this family, don't we? The twins, in the middle of the holiday blizzard. Little Tyler, coming into the family. And now this. You got yourself a father."

Bobby lay in the bed. His skin was pale and his hair mussed. Vidalia smoothed it with one hand, thinking he'd be embarrassed to be seen looking like an upset rooster. "Are you very mad at me, Selene, for not telling you sooner?"

Selene kept her eyes on Bobby's face as well. "You didn't really know."

"I had an inkling."

"Things happen the way they're supposed to, Mom. Everything worked out just fine. And I love you even more knowing you haven't always been perfect."

"I've never even been close."

"You have a giant family out there who'd argue that one." Selene leaned in and kissed her cheek, she wobbled a little on her feet.

"That's it, daughter. Back into bed you go. Come on now." Turning Selene around, Vidalia helped her back to her bed, which was right beside Bobby's. She helped her sit on the edge, then picked up her legs for her, and tucked the covers over her. Her light blue eyes kept falling closed, then popping open over and over, before she even hit the pillow. "I love you, Mama."

"I love you too, Selene. You rest now."

"He's gonna be okay. You don't have to worry," she said, finally letting her eyes fall closed and stay that way. "I talked to my guides. He's gonna be just fine."

"And he'll probably start dancing under the moonlight, what with your marrow in him now."

Selene's lips curved upward, but just barely. "That would be so cool." Then she was asleep, and she needed it. Vidalia patted her hands, then turning, went to stand beside Bobby's bedside.

To her surprise, his eyes were open when she looked at him.

"Well, hello cowboy. You finally decide to wake up?"

He moved his lips, made a face. Vidalia got the water from the bedside, and held its straw near his lips. "Just a little now," she told him.

He sipped, then let his head fall back onto the pillows. "I'm sorry, Vidalia. I thought...I thought there would be...more time."

"Oh, there is. There's lots more time. Take a good long look at the girl in the next bed, will you Bobby Joe?" And she stepped aside as she said it.

Bobby turned his head, then he frowned harder. "Is that your Selene?"

"Turns out she's actually...your Selene too."

"She...?"

"Bobby, she's yours. The doc told us you needed bone marrow and that none of your boys were a match. Why on earth didn't you say something when I told you she might be yours?"

"I didn't want to know so I could take her bone marrow, woman. I wanted to spend time with her, while I still had time to spend." Then he blinked, tearing his eyes from the sleeping blonde and fixing them on Vidalia again.

"Selene...?"

"Is a perfect match. And so you, my love, are cured. Oh, the doc is making noises about having to keep you alive long enough for the new bone marrow to start doing its job, but I have my sources and Selene has hers, and they both agree, you're gonna be fine."

"I'm not dying?"

"Not anytime soon," she told him.

"Are you...sure?"

She looked past him briefly, then got stuck there, her eyes on the window. "I am now."

He looked where she was looking.

Soft snowflakes fell past the darkened window, dancing and spinning as they drifted to the ground. "It's Christmas," she told him. "It's snowing. And you're alive."

He dragged his stunned eyes back to hers again, as, from just outside the doors, a group of voices sang Silent Night in perfect four part harmony. They sounded just like angels.

Then his hand moved, as if in search of his pockets, only he no longer had any. "Your present. I had it in my pocket."

"I know." She pulled it out of her own pocket. "I thought it might be for me, but I didn't look. I wanted to wait for you."

He took the tiny box from her, and turning it to face him, he opened it. "When I came back here, I thought my time was running out. And I made a decision to live what was left of my life doing what was important. Doing what was right. I wanted to spend my time with my boys, building something I could leave behind for them. And I wanted to spend it with you, basking in you the way I should have been doing all along."

He gripped the bed's rail and shook it. "Lower this danged thing, will you?"

"You're not getting up!"

"Gonna start bossing me around already, woman? Lower it or I'll climb over. I'm gonna do this right."

She lowered the rail. He sat up, put his legs over the side, and then pushed off the mattress before she was even ready. His feet hit the floor, his knees bent, and he went down onto them so fast she couldn't stop him.

"Mr. McIntyre!" a nurse shouted.

He held up one hand and sent her a silencing look. Then he lifted his head, and the little black box, its lid open now, the ring winking and twinkling inside. "Sweet Vidalia, you are the love of my life, and I refuse to live another day without you. Will you marry me?"

Her tears were streaming. The carolers had just broken into the third verse in the hallway, and even the nurse was sniffling.

"Say yes, Mom," Selene whispered. "Make me legitimate."

Vidalia dropped to her knees too, pressed her hands to Bobby's cheeks, and kissed his mouth slowly. When she finished, she spoke so close her lips brushed his as she told him, "You bet I will."

He grinned, plucked the ring from the box and slipped it onto her finger. A loud cheer broke out, and they both turned their heads to see a number of faces vying for a spot outside the door's glass windows, her daughters and his sons, all of them smiling so wide it was blinding.

They kissed again, kneeling there in front of the window with the snowflakes as their backdrop, and Vidalia knew that her fondest wish, her very own Christmas miracle, had been delivered right then, that very night, on the Christmas when her life began anew.

-The End-

If you enjoyed The Oklahoma Brands,
continue reading for an excerpt from
Oklahoma Christmas Blues,
the first book in The Bliss in Big Falls series.

OKLAHOMA CHRISTMAS BLUES

*T*he Long Branch Saloon didn't open for another hour, but how could anyone resist Santa Claus peering through the window, tapping on the glass?

Sophia wiped her hands on a bar towel and went to let him in, and he beamed a smile at her. His dimples were very real, and so, she thought, was his snowy white beard. "Chilly out there today," he said. "I brought my lunch, but I'm craving a hot cocoa to go with it."

"Hot cocoa it is."

"I'll take it to go," he said, looking around. "You're not open yet, are you?"

"Not quite. I'm just getting familiar with the layout. My first day on the job and all."

"Ah, and here I thought I recognized you. You're new in town?"

"Sure am," she said. "I grew up in a small town a lot like this one, though." At seventeen, she'd thought she couldn't shake the dust of her hometown off her boots fast enough. At twenty-nine and counting (loudly, inside her head), she'd come running to Big Falls, Oklahoma like her tail was on fire. Her dream life had crumbled. This small town was the only place where she had family these days. Coming here had been a knee-jerk reaction, an impulse. Whether it had been a good one remained to be seen.

"Sophia McIntyre," she said, extending a hand. Santa pulled off his thin white gloves and clasped her hand in his. It was warm and strong. "You just find a comfortable stool, Santa. You can eat your lunch right here where it's warm. I'll get that cocoa."

She went behind the bar and took down one of the heavy stoneware mugs. "Marshmallows?"

"Absolutely."

Smiling, Sophia mixed and stirred and dropped some marshmallows on top, then set the mug full of chocolate in front of her first customer. Santa pressed his palms to the mug and, closing his eyes, inhaled the steam. "Mmm. Simple pleasures."

She couldn't reply, not having had many of those lately.

"Are you a bartender by trade, Sophie?"

"Sophia," she corrected. "Time will tell, I guess." He frowned at her, but waited for more, and she found herself talking though she didn't know why. "I worked my way through college and med school slinging drinks. It's like riding a bike. You never forget."

"So you're a doctor then? My, my. Small-town girl makes good." She didn't reply, but he went on. "What brings you to Big Falls?"

She shrugged. "I have family here. I don't know, it seemed like the best place to be while waiting to hear whether my license will be pulled for the creative way my ex-fiancé was using my prescription pad."

"Oh dear." He reached across the bar to pat her hand. "I'm sorry to hear that, Sophie."

She glanced up at him, shook her head. "Maybe it's not like

riding a bike. I think you're supposed to be telling me your problems, aren't you, Santa?"

"Oh, I don't have problems. There are no such things, you know."

"No such things as problems?" She lifted her head, met his impossibly blue eyes.

"Absolutely not. Nothing happens *to* you. Everything happens *for* you. That's what I always say. Everything that comes along is designed to help you get where you're supposed to be. If you ask me, you're supposed to be right here. You didn't know it, so life gave you a little nudge."

He sipped his cocoa, his elbow on the bar. She'd seen him from a distance yesterday, when she'd first arrived. She'd been driving her Subaru real slow through downtown Big Falls. He'd been in the park that Main Street encircled, holding court in the pavilion on a red velvet throne. Now that he was up close, her memory tried to tell her he was the same Santa who'd been in her own small town when she'd been a little girl. For just a second, she was eight years old again, sitting on his knee, looking up at him with wonder in her eyes.

But that wasn't very likely, was it? No. Not even possible, really.

"Maybe, Sophie, everything you really want is right here in Big Falls, waiting for you. Maybe you don't belong in New York City after all."

"It's Sophia," she corrected again. *Sophia* was successful, respected and wealthy. *Sophie* was just a country girl with big dreams. And then she said, "You really believe that? A fiancé who's dealing drugs on the side? A criminal investigation and my medical license in jeopardy? All that's happening *for* me?"

He shrugged, sipped, studied her. "What if it was?"

She frowned, starting to think this Santa Claus was, perhaps, suffering from the onset of dementia. Poor thing.

"No, no, hear me out now," he said, just as if he'd heard her thoughts. "Santa knows these things. What if all those recent events happened because your true calling, your true happiness, the life of your dreams, is right here in Big Falls?"

She frowned, tilting her head to one side and looking into his eyes. "I wish that was true."

"Don't wish it." He leaned back a little, sipped his cocoa and put his mug down. There was chocolate decorating the edges of his whiskers. "I think for right now you ought to try *hoping* it. Just hope, even if only for the next few days, that everything in your life is happening exactly the way it's supposed to. You might be surprised." He smiled, and chugged the rest of his cocoa. "Gotta run, Sophie. Children are waiting." Then he slid off his stool and reached into the pocket of his red velvet coat.

Sophia held up her hands. "No. Your money's no good here, Santa."

"Thank you." He smiled at her and something flashed in his eyes, a full blown twinkle so unexpected she took a step backwards in shock. "Believe the way you believed when you were a little girl, and watch the magic happen. Lots of magic around, especially this time of year." Then he winked, turned and walked away.

Sophie—Sophia—stared at the batwing doors long after he'd gone through them. She didn't quite know what to make of the Santa who maybe believed a little too much. And yet she couldn't get what he'd said out of her mind.

What if her life hadn't just disintegrated by chance, or bad luck, or because fate had it in for her? What if there was a *reason*? And how the heck did he know she was from New York?

Small town grapevine. Had to be.

Her three cousins, the hunks she referred to as the McIntyre men, showed up to open the Long Branch for the evening, and she fell into the rhythm of pouring, stirring, blending. She used to be very good at this job, and in no time, it was all coming back to her. She could flip a bottle in the air, spin around, catch it and pour it, all in one move. She started having fun. People were fond of her uncle Bobby Joe, who'd built this saloon, and the family he'd married into, the Brands. He and his wife since last Christmas, Vidalia, came in to watch her work and made a big fuss about how good she was at the job. They'd insisted she stay in their guest room while she was in town. They made her feel welcome. Wanted. They acted like hosting her for the holidays was a gift to them.

A warm feeling started to settle over her. A comfortable feeling. A feeling of...*home*. She hadn't had that feeling since she'd left her own small town all those years ago, after her mom had died. She hadn't even known how much she'd missed that feeling of home, of family.

Maybe that crazy old Santa had a point. Maybe she needed to keep an open mind.

When she got back to the farmhouse, it was late. She hadn't expected to find anyone awake, and went in quietly, so she wouldn't wake anyone up. The place was illuminated by the Christmas lights that twinkled from a huge Douglas fir in the living room and the soft glow of the fireplace. The smell of freshly baked cookies made the air almost taste of chocolate. As she tiptoed through the living room, she spotted Aunt Vidalia in a rocking chair in front of the fire. She was sealing an envelope and she looked up, smiling when she saw her. "Oh, good, you're home," she said. "I saved you a cookie. It's probably still warm." She nodded toward a plate that held a giant cookie. It was on an end table right beside a giant, soft easy chair.

Unable to resist, Sophia sank into that chair. "You're going to spoil me so much I'll never want to leave," she said. The fire crackled and the tree twinkled. She inhaled the mingled scents of evergreen and burning wood, and a hint of peppermint from somewhere.

"That's the plan." Vidalia got up and set her envelope on the mantle.

Sophia couldn't help but notice the name scrawled across the front. *Santa.* She frowned, looking at her aunt again.

Vidalia shrugged. "I write to him every year. Leave the letter on the mantle. On Christmas Eve, put out some cookies and milk. And you know, throughout the coming year, most of the things I put in the letter come to me."

Sophia smiled and said, "Like…a new set of cookie sheets, or a pretty new nightgown?"

"Oh, sweetie, I wouldn't waste my letter to Santa on such trivial things. No, I'm talking about big things. Healthy grand-babies, happy daughters, the love of my life." Smiling wistfully, she crossed the room, picking up her pad of candy cane bordered stationary and her red ink pen on the way, and then she offered them both to Sophia. "You should give it a try."

"What is it with this town and Santa Claus?" she muttered.

Vidalia crooked a dark brow. "You have a problem with Santa Claus?"

Sophia grinned at the intensity in her aunt's eyes. "Not on your life. Gimme that pen and pad."

She took both, said good night to Vidalia, and nibbled on her cookie. And then she sat there, alone in the living room in front of the giant, twinkling Christmas tree, and she did something she hadn't done in twenty years. She wrote a letter to Santa Claus.

Dear Santa,

If it's true what you told me, then that would be…amazing. So amazing that I think I have to give it a try. I'm going to hope that maybe everything that's happening to me is for a reason and that it's sending me toward the life I want. I'm going to hope. What do I have to lose? And I figure I need to get clear on what to hope for. So, Santa Claus, here's the life I want. I want....

There she paused as a million things ran through her mind. What did she want? She wanted her ex-fiancé Skyler in jail. But that was already a given. He'd been convicted of using her prescription pad to obtain OxyContin and then selling it to addicts. He was only free until his sentencing right after the holidays. The problem was he wouldn't leave her alone. She wasn't afraid of him. But he kept calling and when she changed her number, emailing, and when she blocked his email, coming over to her duplex and pounding on her door and not leaving until she called the police. After the third time, she'd stopped sleeping at night.

It was the pounding on the door part that had made her decide to leave New York. She didn't want anything more to do with Skyler. She just wanted peace.

Nodding, Sophia picked up her pen and wrote, *I want such a peaceful, serene life that I sleep like a baby every night.*

That was a good start. What else, what else?

I want my good name cleared, the investigation closed, the police to believe I had nothing to do with any of it. And I want the Medical Review Board to find the same thing. Vindication, that's what I want.

Her only crime, she thought, had been being a little too naive. A little too hopeful. A little too trusting. She'd had everything she'd ever wanted. A seemingly-decent man who wanted to marry her. A respectable position in an elite hospital's oncology department. A crazy salary.

But even with all that, she hadn't been happy. She'd been beating herself up for it, too, berating herself for what seemed illogical. Why not be happy when she had everything she'd ever wanted? What was wrong with her?

Nodding hard, she realized that despite feeling she *should* be happy, she truly hadn't been. And she wanted to be. So she wrote, *I want happiness, true, deep, lasting joy in my life.*

Nodding, she decided this felt really good, this exercise in hope. And she thought maybe she shouldn't have been so hard on herself before. How could she have been happy in the state she'd been in back then? Even before Skyler's arrest and the subsequent revelations. Her job was stressful and depressing. She'd been tied up in knots all the time and hadn't even known it. Not until those knots had started to untie themselves.

The drive back to Oklahoma had been like a full-body massage. Her tight muscles felt looser and looser the closer she got. And when she'd stepped out of the car at Bobby Joe and Vidalia's farmhouse just outside of town, she'd been compelled to heel off her shoes and sink her feet into the grass. She'd taken a deep breath and felt a thousand pounds just ease off her shoulders.

That certainly lent credence to Santa's theory that she belonged here.

Her career was back in New York, true enough. But she did not want to return to the tension she'd been living, unaware. She didn't know what she was supposed to do.

Nodding, she bent over her letter and added, *I want clarity. I want to know what it is I'm supposed to be doing with my life and I want it to be something that I love, using my skills, but without all the stress and tension I had before.*

This was good. Her letter was coming along beautifully. But there was one last thing, the obvious one, and the most difficult. She wanted love. She wanted the kind of love she saw between Bobby Joe and Vidalia. Uncle Bobby Joe was more relaxed and happier than she'd ever seen him. He looked ten years younger. Vidalia, a raven-haired beauty of Mexican descent, who had cheekbones to die for, obviously adored him. She had five grown daughters and would make Sophia number six if she'd let

her. She was the living proof that fifty-something was the new thirty-something. Sophia had loved her on sight.

The two of them together were...it just was amazing to watch. They interacted like cogs in a wheel, like they were sharing a brain, and they were a unit that was far more than the sum of its parts. It was supernatural, the power of what was between them. Damn, she wanted that.

To think she'd been about to settle for something that wasn't even close. What a narrow escape!

Nodding, she added it to her letter.

"I want love," she whispered as she wrote the words down. "I want true, deep, crazy, passionate, beautiful, heart-racing, soul-filling, breathtaking love, Santa. And you know what else? I really don't want to go through the holidays without someone special to share them with." And then she wrote a little more. *I'm going to try hoping this really works, just like you said, Santa. And if it doesn't, you're never getting free cocoa from the Long Branch again.*

And then she signed it. *Love, Sophie.*

Frowning, she looked down at what she'd written, surprised to find that she'd written Sophie, and not Sophia. She started to try to make the *e* into an *a*, but something made her stop. She put the pen down. Then picked it up again and added, *PS. Just kidding about the free cocoa.*

Then she folded the letter and tucked it into a plain white envelope. But she didn't leave it on the mantle or seal the envelope. There were a couple of days until Christmas, and she might just need to edit it.

She held her letter to her chest, closed her eyes and said, "Okay, Santa. Here goes nothing. I really, really hope this works. Ball's in your court, big guy. Bring on the magic."

Oklahoma Christmas Blues

ALSO AVAILABLE

The Oklahoma Brands
The Brands who Came for Christmas
Brand-New Heartache
Secrets and Lies
A Mommy For Christmas
One Magic Summer
Sweet Vidalia Brand

The McIntyre Men
Oklahoma Christmas Blues
Oklahoma Moonshine
Oklahoma Starshine
Shine On Oklahoma
Baby By Christmas
Oklahoma Sunshine

www.ingramcontent.com/pod-product-compliance
Lightning Source LLC
Chambersburg PA
CBHW011519100726
47899CB00010BD/3440